GW00390876

THANK YOU so much for buying this book!

Tornado

Savage Brotherhood MC: Book One

A Paranormal Romance

By Jasmine Wylder

Chapter One
Ava

"Ugh, what a night!" Ava dramatically threw herself over the table in the back of the café where she worked. She glanced at her friend and coworker, Melanie. "I need a drink."

Melanie had her shoes off, resting her feet from her ten-hour shift. She and Ava had come on together. The other feline shifter was literally the only thing that had kept her sane today.

It had been a rough day, with picky customer after picky customer coming in and asking for drinks that seemed to take an entire sentence to describe. Ava had only been working at the coffee shop for six months, but it had felt like a lifetime—she absolutely hated every moment of it.

"Wanna hit the bar with me?" Ava arched her brow at Melanie. "We haven't gone to that one near my place."

Melanie frowned. "That weird little hole-in-the-wall? The place that doesn't even have a sign? That's a bad idea, Ava. That place is full of that *gang*."

Ava saw the worry starting to creep in around the edges of Melanie's eyes, and waved it off with a laugh. "Fine then, no bar. I think I've got a couple beers at home. We could just chill out."

Her friend's expression cleared and she smiled. "Fraid not, Ava. Sorry. I'm exhausted. Maybe next time."

"Sure thing."

The two women hugged each other. In a town as small as Coalfell, it was difficult to find shifters who weren't associated with the Savage Brotherhood, a motorcycle club, and doubly hard to find feline shifters. Ava's own panther had picked up Melanie's feline scent when they first met, though it had taken several months before the other shifter opened up to her.

Ava waved to her other coworkers as she left and headed out to her car. She was almost there when a strange scent hit her nostrils. She wrinkled her nose as she glanced around, trying to locate the source of the scent.

A man stood on the other side of the parking lot. He was tall, thin, and pale. Even across the lot, his gaze seemed to pierce right through her. Seeing her staring at him, he smiled at her in a way that didn't quite match his features, as if smiling was unnatural for him.

She froze, keys in her hand. Her panther hissed, and the hair stood up on the back of her neck.

The man slid into the car next to him and drove away. The sickly-sweet scent lingered, making Ava's stomach churn. Her hands trembling, she quickly got into her car and took off out of the parking lot. She dealt with a lot of creeps, but nobody had managed to unsettle her panther with a single glance like that.

As she passed the seedy little bar on her way home, her mind flashed to Melanie's warning. But her hands were still trembling, and she knew she needed something stronger than beer to calm her nerves tonight.

Ever since she had moved to her new house, she had been looking forward to exploring this little hole in the wall. It was the kind of place that always had motorcycles parked out front no matter what time of year. A barely-lit sign that was small and almost unnoticeable announced it was a bar.

It wasn't the kind of bar that you went to if you hadn't already been there before, but Ava wasn't intimidated. "Gang", Melanie called them. Coalfell was little more than a spit of a town. They only had one traffic light, for God's sake! She wasn't afraid of a bunch of tough guy posers with Mom tattoos.

If there was one thing she was completely certain of, it was that she didn't scare easily. And after her unnerving encounter—it wasn't even an encounter—with the pale man, she needed to prove that again.

She turned into the parking lot, edging into the end beside a sweet looking ride with red flames painted over it.

The smell of cigarette smoke completely overrode the smell of her coffee and sweat as she stepped inside, although the town had banned smoking inside years ago. Ava wasn't surprised to find out that this place was the kind that would disregard that rule.

The whole place was dimly-lit, the only light from small lamps above the tables and an overhead light at the bar. Several patrons nudged each other and leered at her, but she ignored them as she sat at the bar. The bartender wore a dirty flannel shirt, with an even dirtier apron wrapped around his waist.

He eyed her in an unfriendly manner. "What you want?"

Ava didn't let herself get intimidated by the gruff question. "I'd like—"

"Les." A man two stools down slid a glass across the bar. "Get me another."

The bartender turned away at once. Ava glared at the man who'd ordered the drink.

"Didn't your mother ever tell you it's rude to interrupt people?"

The man turned his face to her, raising an eyebrow. He was handsome, with dark, thick hair in a mess on his head, blue eyes, a heavy brow, and sharp, high cheekbones that were accented by the light at the bar. The sleeves of his shirt were pushed up to the elbows, revealing sleeve tattoos on both arms.

He eyed her. "Didn't your mother ever tell you it's dangerous for a pretty girl to come to a bar all by her lonesome?"

"No," Ava spat back at once and gave him a sugary smile. "She taught me how to rip out men's throats."

Les gave her a look as though she was crazy as he handed the man a new drink. Several of the other patrons snickered, and Ava realized she had an audience. An uncomfortable prickling swept over her arms until the man smiled at her.

"Relax, everybody. This pretty kitten's here to stay."

There was a tangible relaxation to the air and everybody turned back to what they were doing. The man moved to a closer seat and gestured at the bartender.

"Anything she wants, Les. On my tab."

"I can pay for my own drinks," Ava snapped. She sucked in a deep breath, struggling to calm herself down. Her panther was all puffed up, hissing, but not in the way that usually foretold danger; it was just annoyed. "Give me whiskey."

Les glanced between the two of them and pulled a bottle off the top shelf.

"Not that stuff, something down there."

Les chuckled. "Boss says it's on his tab, it's on his tab. So top shelf it is."

He poured her the shot and she stared at the amber liquid for a moment before taking a deep breath, holding it as she drank the liquor down in one swallow. The burn made her cough, but she waved for Les to refill her glass.

She could feel the man's eyes on her, like a caress on her skin. There was something about him that piqued her animal senses, something that she could feel in her core. She shot a look at him.

"Boss, huh? You own this place?"

He only grinned at her. "What's it to you, Kitten? What's your deal?"

His voice was rich and smooth—charming, which annoyed her deeply. She didn't say anything. She sipped her new whiskey, looking over at him. She found that it was hard to take her eyes off of his face, the lines of his jaw and his lips.

He cocked his head and shrugged. "Ok, don't talk. There's only one reason why a sweet little feline like you would come to the armpit of Satan that is Coalfell. So, what is it? Boyfriend found out you're a shifter and left you?"

All color drained from her face. "Wh-what?"

"Don't play games." His voice took on a harder edge. "You're a shifter. I can smell the wild on you. Am I wrong?"

Her eyes widened as she turned towards him, her heart in her throat. So far Melanie was the only shifter in town she'd met. And back where she used to live... well, it was always drilled into her to hide what she was. Humans wouldn't understand.

"You're one, too?" she whispered.

The man laughed. "We're all shifters here. Right boys?"

Everybody in the bar cheered, lifting their glasses. One woman, a brunette with half her head shaved, rolled her eyes. She didn't speak, though. Ava felt herself relax further. A whole bar of shifters? No wonder they kept this place so uninviting. They didn't want humans to stumble in and ruin their fun.

The man suddenly seized her hand. "Come with me."

It wasn't a request. It was a command. Something spun giddily down Ava's spine, but she snorted, removed her hand from his, and finished her drink before she stood.

He didn't wait another moment. He seized her hand again and pulled her through a side door, into the dirty alley behind the bar. It was cold outside, but the cool breeze felt good on her skin.

He turned to her, eyes alight. He gestured to a bit of forest she'd been longing to explore since she arrived. "Show me yours and I'll show you mine."

Now that there wasn't the cigarette smoke messing with her nose, she could smell him. Deep and rich, earthy but clean. Like cinnamon and spice. Such a strange combination for such a huge, intimidating man.

She swallowed, considering it for a moment. She hadn't shifted into her panther form in months, and she knew how good it would feel to do it.

"You know what I think?" she put her hands on her hips. She had always been blessed with a curvy figure, and this outfit clung to her breasts while minimizing her waist. Her panties started getting damp as she thought about what he must intend for her. "I think you're just trying to get me naked."

He grinned at her. "Something wrong with that?"

He had stripped off his shirt before she could reply. Her mouth instantly became dry as she saw his hard abs. The contours of his chest, the smooth lines of his biceps. His tattoos went all the way to his shoulders. Ava caught the sight of two faces on his pec over his heart before he started to pull off his pants.

She whirled, determined not to stand there staring like an idiot, and tugged her dress off over her head. Part of her wanted to see if he was checking her out, but she refused to give him that satisfaction. She kicked off her shoes and removed her underwear before shifting.

Her muscles stretched as she dug her claws into the dirty asphalt. Oh *yes*. It felt good to be in her panther's skin again.

She turned and faced the biggest wolf she had ever seen. He definitely outweighed her in their animal forms and was taller, too. Green eyes peered from grey fur, studying her.

Ava leaned in to sniff him, unable to stop herself. The spice scent was even stronger now. He sniffed her as well, nuzzling her neck, breathing her in as they studied each other. He nipped at her throat playfully and she lifted her paw, batting at him as excitement coursed through her.

His tail swung from side to side, and he slapped the ground with his two front paws then bounded into the woods. Ava chased after him, her ears pricked up. Blood rushed through her, heating her even as the night air grew cooler.

He was larger, but she was faster. When she caught up with him, she jumped on his back, knocking him to the ground. His paws wrapped around her and he suddenly twisted, rolling her to the ground. He leaned down and nuzzled her jaw as she laid on her back. She batted at him again. They wrestled around, biting and teasing each other.

With a sudden yelp, he was off again. Ava dashed after him, the moon in the sky and the shadows fleeing before their play. Eventually, they both came to a stop in a mossy clearing. The wolf flopped to his side on the ground. Ava admired the way his fur gleamed in the moonlight. Then, she took a few steps toward him, before lowering herself to the ground and curling up next to him.

For a few moments, they just lay there comfortably, Ava enjoying the warmth of him, the feeling of her body close to his. Hours seemed to pass as they stayed there nuzzling each other, biting and gently playing.

He flipped her onto her back, his big wolf body slowly morphing back to that well-defined face. With the moon behind him, all she could see was the glitter in his eyes. She heard his panting, though, and before she even knew what she was doing, she had shifted back to her human form beneath him.

He came to her then, taking her face in his hands before leaning in to kiss her softly on the lips. He held her there, sucking on her lips until she started to respond. Electricity flowed through her at the touch of his mouth. Ava wrapped her arms around his neck, tasting him, the kiss growing hungry and deep within just a few seconds.

His body pressed against hers and a snarl came from her lips. He chuckled and pulled back.

"You," he said against her lips. "You are the sweetest thing I've ever tasted."

Ava's breath was ragged, caught in her throat. He kissed her again, his tongue slipping between her lips to tease her own. He brought his mouth to her ear, then, kissing just below it.

"What does the rest of you taste like?" he asked.

She moved her thighs to either side of his hips and gave him a wicked grin. "Only one way to find out... *Boss*."

Hunger flared in his eyes and he kissed her again, long and deep, before exploring the rest of her body with his hands and mouth. She was near helpless under his touch, never having felt something so explosive before. The forest disappeared around her until it was just her and him and nothing else.

When they were both finished and panting, he stretched and sighed. "Ah, yes. I needed that. Thanks, Kitten. Too bad it's over."

She caressed his chest with her lips. "You could come back to my place and—"

"No. I don't usually make a habit of sticking around with the women I fuck. Sorry."

Fuck. *Fuck.* Ava felt her words sticking in her throat. They had run in the moonlight, played together, and shared one another's bodies. She hadn't felt this free in... well, ever. And he said *fuck*. The crude way he said it stung and she pulled away from him, especially after how connected she had felt to him in her animal form.

"What? We fucked, didn't we?"

Ava's nostrils flared. "I don't know why I'm surprised. I knew that you were a pig from the moment I met you."

Something flashed in his eyes. "What are you talking about? You thought I was a pig, and that's why you let me *fuck* you?"

Now he was doing it just to upset her. She snarled, her panther's claws sharpening. "Well, I hope you enjoyed it. 'Cause you're never touching this *kitten* again."

"Should have known you'd be one of *those* women." The wolf groaned. "You go to a bar like that to get picked up, don't act like this was some sort of—"

"Shut up!" she shouted. To her humiliation, tears sprang to her eyes.

She sprang to her feet, shifted, and tore off into the forest.

Chapter Two
Jackson

Jackson walked back to his bike where it was parked at the bar, filled with irritation and annoyance at the woman he had just met. He hadn't gotten her name, but it seemed that he'd gotten to know every part of her, every part that she was willing to show him.

He heard the merriment coming from the bar but didn't want to deal with them right now. Not when the panther's scent was all over him. Why was guilt twisting in his gut? He had made sure she got home safe. It wasn't like he'd left her running around the forest by herself. There was nothing else he was supposed to do with a casual hookup.

A sweet little kitten like that wouldn't be able to handle his life. There was no reason for that hurt look on her face to linger in his mind any longer.

Yet, when he started his bike, he angled it towards her house, wanting to apologize for being so crude with her at the end. Even if she shouldn't have expected anything other than a one-time thing. She had awoken his wolf in a way that had never happened before, making it playful. He couldn't remember the last time he *played*.

The light was on in her home and the door was slightly ajar. When he turned off his bike and headed for the door, he caught a sickly-sweet scent. Rotting sugar. A chill ran up his spine and he dashed inside. A muffled scream met his ears, and, with a roar, he launched himself into the room it was coming from.

The panther crouched on the floor. Beside her stood a man he had never wanted to see again. Astrophel's eyes glowed as he whipped a hand across the panther's face. She fell back with a small cry.

Jackson lunged at Astrophel as he started to bend over the panther, but the vampire threw back his elbow, hitting Jackson's chest. The wind was knocked out of him and he stumbled back. Astrophel lunged, sinking teeth into the panther's shoulder.

"No!" The cry was ripped from him before he could stop it.

Jackson choked on his breath, trying to catch it as he shifted into his wolf form and lunged at the vampire. Astrophel fell to the ground, cursing, then got to his feet unnaturally fast. He glided backward, floating just above the ground.

"Stay your attack, Son of the Storm."

Jackson itched to launch himself at the vampire again but stopped himself. Astrophel was one of the oldest, most powerful vampire kings. Killing him would only cause disaster. His skin prickled as the panther whimpered on the floor, but he forced himself to shift back to human form.

"She is one of mine. You know the rules; you're allowed humans that stray into your territory," and that was only because it would be a massacre, for both humans and shifters, if they tried to starve out the vampires, "but coming into Savage territory is—"

"Is forbidden, yes, yes." Astrophel waved a hand, looking bored. "You also know that if one of your shifters kills one of my vampires, I am permitted my choice among your people."

A shiver ran down Jackson's spine as Astrophel pulled a cellphone from his pocket. He swiped his thumb over it and tossed it to Jackson. The image of a shifter savaging a vampire came onto the screen. Jackson swiped through a few more images, until the shifter ripped off the head of the vampire he was fighting.

"He's not one of mine," Jackson snarled as he tossed the phone back.

Astrophel rose a brow. "No?"

"No." His heart slammed hard into his chest. "Do not disrespect the treaty. You know how this works, corpse. You don't mess with us, we don't kill every single one of your kind."

The treaty, the Contract of Peace, governed how vampires and shifters interacted with each other. Mostly, it involved staying away from each other, but lately there had been more vampire attacks on both shifters and humans on the borders. Some people, like the shifter that had attacked the vampire in the woods, were talking of taking matters into their own hands.

"The treaty," Astrophel repeated. "By its writings, I can claim any shifter life in exchange for the life that was taken from my people. Do not disrespect the treaty, dog. Is this *kitten* worth your risks?"

The panther whimpered. She was still conscious? Jackson's hands clenched. He should tell the vampire to take her and go. What was she? A casualty to the war. She never should have been involved in this, sure, but she was not worth sacrificing more lives over.

His jaw clenched as his wolf growled. He would never give up so easily.

Astrophel sighed and shrugged. "You cannot save her, boy. When she's a raging beast, bring her to the cave where you watched your parents die. I will take my claim there."

Jackson lunged, but Astrophel had already leapt out the window, glass shattering around him. The vampire's form darkened and disappeared into the sky.

He moved to follow, but a whimper behind him made him turn. The panther stared at him with wide eyes, her dark hair tumbled around her shoulders. One hand pressed tight to her shoulder as blood dripped between her fingers.

"Fuck," Jackson hissed, dropping to his knees next to her.

"Don't—" she gasped. "Don't say that word."

Her eyes rolled into her head and she collapsed. Jackson was just able to catch her before she hit the floor. Her hand dropped, revealing what he had been dreading. Astrophel's green venom, stinking of death, bubbled at the edges of her wound.

It didn't always happen, but vampire venom was more than capable of killing shifters. With humans, it was different. Humans got a high from vampire venom and were able to be turned.

He tore open her dress and focused on the wound. Fresh. There was a chance. He dropped over her, locking his lips over the bite mark, and started to suck, trying to draw the venom out. It burned on his tongue and tasted like rotten meat, but he fought down the gag reflex and continued.

He wasn't sure how long he sucked before the putrid taste was replaced by clean blood. He spat out the mouthful, checking her pulse. Fever burned her skin, her breathing was shallow, but her heart beat was strong.

The trickle of blood slowed to an ooze, and he nodded, satisfied that she was healing. Soft whimpers came from her lips as he pulled her into his arms. They couldn't stay here. And with Astrophel having staked his claim, there was only one place for him to take her.

***

His sister's eyes were cold and angry when she pulled up in a stolen minivan. Her nostrils flared when he pulled the panther into the vehicle, but Val didn't say anything as she peeled out of the neighborhood. Gratitude welled up in him. Anybody else would be questioning him, but not Val.

She was silent as she drove to the safehouse. The old building seemed like something Norman Bates would live in, a two-story house that would otherwise be called a cabin. It was located deep in the woods beyond the city, away from any man-made path in the forest. Val slipped the key in the door and pushed it open, then stood back to allow Jackson in. He carried Ava in, greeted by a new kind of still, stuffy coldness, and laid her on the couch. He touched her skin to find it was no longer warm, but cold and clammy.

He sat next to her and pulled her into his lap to give her some warmth. "Find some blankets."

"Like hell, Tornado."

It had been a while since she called him that. Everybody in the gang had a nickname, but Val usually called him by his name. The only one who did.

"I can smell vampire on her. What happened?"

Jackson glared at her.

"You know this safe house is only for the gang. Only for us. When Typhoon finds out you brought an infected here, he's going to kill you. And since he's not touching you without going through me..." She narrowed her eyes. "Tell me what happened."

His jaw tightened for a moment before he sighed. "A shifter killed a vamp."

Val hissed between her teeth. "Shit!"

"Astrophel has claimed her as payment."

"Give her to him."

Jackson's wolf growled, the sound reverberating from his throat.

"What's she worth? Not the lives of our men." Val narrowed her eyes at him. "Jackson. She's not worth it."

"The guy who killed the vamp wasn't one of our guys. The treaty isn't broken. Astrophel should have dealt with the alphas, rather than coming into my territory and claiming one of my people."

"She's not one of your people, she's an outsider!"

"She's a shifter!" Jackson roared, causing the panther to flinch. He sucked in a deep breath and eased her back to the couch. He towered over his sister and narrowed his eyes at her. "She stays."

Val glared for a moment before she dropped her gaze and backed up a step. "Fine. Whatever. But you know this house won't hold if Astrophel and his guard show up. Not to mention she was bitten. Tie her up, and when she goes mad maybe you'll hand her over to the corpse."

"No."

"Great," said Val sarcastically. "Now you've got a monster on your hands and a vamp out for blood."

"It doesn't happen to everyone," Jackson said. Val raised her eyebrows.

"Name a shifter who got bit by a vamp who didn't go rabid after," she said.

Jackson said nothing. He glanced back over his shoulder at the woman, who stirred in her sleep but didn't move, her eyelids only fluttering.

"He only bit her. He didn't drink her blood."

Val studied him for a moment, then nodded again. "You know that they'll take this as an invite, Jackson. You were an idiot to bring her here."

He had to grin at that. His sister never was one to hide her displeasure when she disagreed with him. In private, at least. He could never ask for a more solid lieutenant in the gang.

"I'll take care of her here," he said, ignoring her insult. "If that corpse thinks he's getting his hands on her... There have been more vamp attacks, and with this, him coming onto our territory and claiming a woman just after I..." He frowned for a moment, trying to think of the right word.

"Fucked her?" Val suggested.

kson growled, despite himself.

't like the connotations of that word ght now for some reason. He took a deep breath, shoving that aside. "There's a war coming. We both know it."

"So, what are we going to do, Tornado? You're the boss."

Jackson took a deep breath.

"I'm going to have to think about it. We may need to recruit more people. I have the guys out on a job tonight—"

"Oh, great," Val said. "So, what if something goes wrong, Jackson? And you're at the safe house with a dangerous predator while your guys are out getting busted or worse."

"You can handle it," Jackson said. "Bruno's leading it. Call them back, catch them up. Take care of it. I'm going to—to try to stop her fever."

"You have to tie her up before she wakes up," Val said, shooting him a look.

He didn't look at her, though he knew that it was true. Sometimes, when shifters were infected by vampire venom, they awoke as their animals, wild and out of control. In her panther form, she could kill him with the strength of vampire venom in her blood. He had to tie her up or risk an attack.

"What do we do about the vampires in the meantime?" Val asked as she glanced back at the panther.

Somehow the thought of roping her wrists was not something he wanted to do. She still shivered, and, with a curse, he pulled off his jacket and put it over her.

"Get the rest of the guys on rounds. I want everybody patrolling the perimeter of the city, particularly in the west where that vamp cave is. When Bruno gets back, get him and his crew out here for an extra guard."

Val nodded. She stepped toward the door, then stopped. "Tie her up, Tornado."

He couldn't stop himself from growling this time.

Val's hands clenched, then relaxed. She let out a deep breath and tugged at her dark hair. "Whatever. You do you. But you know I'm going to have to report this to Typhoon. Don't order me not to, or I'll have to tell him that, too."

Jackson nodded reluctantly. "Tell him, then."

"What are you going to do with her?"

"Make her better," Jackson said as he lifted her into his arms. He needed to warm her up first. He'd figure out what to do next after she stopped shivering. "I'll call you in a few days."

"Be careful, Jackson," Val said. "If she wakes up—"

"She won't hurt me," Jackson said.

A strange look came over his sister's face, then she was gone. Jackson shifted the panther's weight in his arms, noting that, despite the situation, her curves molded snugly against him, and carried her down the hall into the bathroom.

It was only after he was running the water almost hot enough to burn that he realized that dunking her in fully clothed was a bad idea. She'd have nothing to wear afterward, and he couldn't have her soaking wet while fighting the venom.

He cursed under his breath and pillowed her head with a towel. Then he found the thermostat and turned it up full blast.

Cleaning out the wound was necessary, though, and hot water was the best way to warm her up quickly. He toyed with his phone, considering calling Val back to help him. He had a feeling that the panther would be less upset about another woman undressing her than a man.

There was no time to argue with her about it, though. Jackson turned his face away as he stripped the waitress' uniform off of the woman's body. He decided to leave on her underwear and lifted her into the hot water. He then held her by the shoulders, making sure that her head stayed above water, while he cleaned out the wound. It was dark and scabbed around the edges, the area red and swollen, but the skin had scabbed over and it no longer bled.

When the bath water started to cool, he lifted her out and wrapped her in several towels. The furnace had kicked in and the house was blazing hot. Jackson carried the panther upstairs, where he toweled down her hair, laid her dress on a chair, and pulled off her soaking underwear.

Not looking at her, he patted her skin dry and then put her into the bed. Color had returned to her cheeks, and, for a moment, he looked at her beneath the blankets, soft and at rest.

He left the room, then, shutting the door quietly, took a deep breath before he begrudgingly locked her inside.

Chapter Three
Ava

Ava groaned when she woke up, her headache splitting her open. The light that beamed in through the window told her that it was morning. She started to stretch when she realized that this wasn't her room. And when she threw back the blankets, she found herself utterly naked.

Panic clawed at her throat. What had happened? She remembered the bar, remembered the wolf... and there had been somebody waiting for her in her home. She remembered nothing after she stepped through the front door.

She glanced around the room. Her bra and panties were nearby, damp as though they had been washed. She frowned but shoved them on before pulling her uniform over her head. Her dress, crusted with blood and torn at the shoulder, gave her a little comfort, but not much.

Taking a deep breath, she padded across the floor to the door. When she tried it, she found it was locked. Ava's heart sank in her chest as she tried it again to no avail.

"Stay focused," she told herself.

She rushed to the window, then. It stuck as she opened it, but she was able to wedge it wide. She found she was on the second floor, with nothing but the steep slope of a roof to slide down if she tried to climb out. A soft laugh came from her throat as she climbed through and jumped out. She willed her panther to come forward, but there was nothing.

She didn't even have time to gasp before she hit the ground, rolling several times.

Pain shot up her ankle and her shoulder throbbed, but Ava didn't care about that. She pushed herself to her knees and placed a hand on her chest. There was no purring from inside, no hissing, no indication that her panther was there at all.

A deep, male voice shouted from behind her. Ava scrambled to her feet and tried to dart into the forest, but more pain shot through her ankle. Her leg wouldn't take her weight and she buckled again. A shadow fell over her and when she looked up, she saw the wolf from last night.

"You!" she shrieked, lunging for him.

He easily dodged her. "What the hell are you doing jumping from a second story window?"

"I know that I'm going to rip your head off with my claws," Ava spat, going for him again.

The wolf sidestepped. A small, amused smile came over his face as he cocked his head and folded his arms. "Glad to know that you still think you can take me, Kitten. You've got a lot of spunk. I think you'll pull through just fine. You're out of danger of going rabid, at least."

Ava's head spun with what he was saying. Or maybe it was more than that. Her stomach revolted against her, but her heaves brought up nothing. When the wolf wrapped his arms around her and hoisted her up, she batted at him, more out of instinct than anything else. Her panther stayed stubbornly missing as he carried her back into the house.

He sat her on the couch, then stepped back and narrowed his eyes. She crossed her arms over her breasts, feeling exposed in her ruined dress.

"Why am I here?" she blurted. The headache, her nausea, and the absence of her panther made her want to collapse, but she wasn't going to do that while he was here. "Because I will tear you in half."

Something in his gaze softened. "I brought you here because you are sick. I'm not planning on—"

"Good," Ava spat. "Don't touch me. I don't want you anywhere near me. I'm going home now."

"No."

"Excuse me?" she asked, her throat dry. "You're—you're going to keep me captive here?"

The wolf rolled his eyes. "You're sick. I can't let you leave when you'll end up dead in a ditch. Now, why don't we stop being irrational and you tell me your name?"

Irrational. *Irrational*? "You kidnapped me, and now you're calling me irrational?"

"I didn't kidnap you," he snapped back. "I saved your life, kitten."

Ava's brow furrowed. She froze when he sat and wrapped his hand around her arm. The familiar tingle of his skin against hers almost made her forget about the whole kidnapping thing.

A hand brushed against her forehead, so gentle she flinched.

The wolf withdrew. The look on his face was concerned, almost... frustrated. Her shoulders relaxed as she accepted that he wasn't there to hurt her. She was confused, but she didn't feel in danger. Otherwise, she would have killed him the moment she got the chance.

"What do you remember from that night?" he asked.

"I remember—running with you," she said. "And—what happened afterward."

"So, you do remember that?" he asked. "When we f—had sex?"

The fact that he censored himself made her eyes widen. He grunted and handed her a blanket, which she wrapped around herself.

"Anything after that?" he asked.

"I went home and there was somebody there. That's it."

"You don't remember Astrophel at all?"

Ava blinked at him. "Who?"

"The vampire," he said, looking into her eyes. "Try to remember."

"Vampire? Are you kidding me?" The disbelief dripped from her tongue.

The wolf rolled his eyes. "Vampire. Blood-sucking, burn-to-ash-in-sunlight vampire. They fly and everything, but they don't turn into bats. That part's just a story. There's a large clan of them that live up in the mountains. Why else do you think there are so many hikers that disappear from around here?"

A shiver ran down Ava's spine. She remembered the pale man, the sense of unease that had filled her when she saw him. She swallowed, trying to wet her throat, but her mouth was dry.

"You're saying I was attacked... by a vampire..."

"Yes. The relationship between the Savage Brotherhood—"

Ava sprang to her feet, only to fall back with a cry. Sweat broke out on her forehead.

"What the fuck?" the wolf looked utterly perplexed.

"You're part of that *gang*," Ava spat out. "Melanie was right, you're going to sell me as a sex slave!"

The wolf's eyes darkened. "We don't do that. There's plenty of crime that we do partake in, but not sex trafficking."

Ava glared at him in response. She knew all about the brothel that one of the other chapters ran over in Ivywood. But the suspicion cleared from her mind as she considered him. No... he wouldn't be part of something like that. She sighed, exhaustion washing over her.

"So, a vampire attacked me."

"Astrophel. He bit you, and the venom will make you sick for a while."

"I feel fine, other than a headache," Ava said. When she focused, she could remember a little bit of the vampire attack. It was the only reason she wasn't completely doubtful. "I suppose I'm a little tired... but I have to go home."

The wolf gripped her wrists, keeping her in place. "He wants you. If you go home, he'll go after you again. But he can't get you here. This place is charmed against vampires. Even a king like Astrophel can't break in unless he brings his whole guard. That would be as good as declaring war on the Brotherhood and they don't have the numbers to take us on. Not to mention that if humans knew about them, they'd nuke the shit out of their mountains."

The wolf gave her a rakish grin which had her heart thumping hard. Ava shivered as the absence of her panther was felt more keenly. She wasn't going to show weakness, though. Even if she was certain he wouldn't hurt her, she wasn't stupid.

"So, what's your name, Kitten?" he asked.

"Ava," she said after a minute.

"Jackson."

A flush rose in her cheeks as she remembered being underneath him, his hardness between her thighs, his lips on her throat. All without even knowing his name. Something twisted in her stomach painfully—whether guilt or her stomach wanting to throw up, she didn't know.

"You're very pale," Jackson took her hand again. "Like I said, you're sick. You'll pull through just fine, but you need to go back to bed. Come on."

Ava didn't find it in herself to protest. Jackson picked her up with ease, earning a little gasp from her, and carried her up the stairs. When he deposited her back on the bed, she almost asked him to lie down with her. Her eyes were *sooo* heavy...

"I'm leaving—after—I wake up," she muttered.

"I'd like to see you try."

She shot him an annoyed look, but the smile on his face made something flutter within her. Her eyes drifted shut, but that smile remained in her mind as sleep overtook her.

***

Fever colored her dreams, and Ava wasn't sure what was real and what was fantasy. Jackson helped her drink soup broth. He carried her to the bathroom and held her upright in the shower, he sat next to her when her eyes fluttered open in the moonlight, he laid cool clothes on her forehead and often talked on the phone, growling and snapping.

The fever seemed to last for days, each day worse than the last.

She wasn't sure how much time went by before she woke in the bright daylight, her mind clear. Considering how close to death she had felt before, she now felt oddly... rested. Like she'd had the sleep of her life, not that she'd been so deathly ill. The room was empty.

"Hello?" she called.

Jackson came then, smiling when he saw her sitting up. Ava stared at him, wondering how long she had been at his house, how much time she'd missed from work.

"How are you?" he asked.

"Hungry," Ava said.

He nodded. "I'll be right back."

He disappeared, and she heard his footsteps on the stairs as he climbed down. A few minutes later, he was back with a tray of food that he put on her lap. Plain toast, some orange juice, and a small cup of applesauce. Not much of a feast, but about all her stomach could take after being so sick. Ava ate slowly, not wanting to throw it up again.

He sat down on the edge of the bed, and Ava stared at him curiously. He'd been caring for her for who knew how long. Why? What was she to him? He didn't strike her as the Florence Nightingale type.

"I think that was the worst of it," he said. "Your fever broke last night, and I think your shifter immune system has kicked back in. You were lucky. It could have been much worse."

"Thank you." Ava smiled hesitantly, though genuinely. "What a way to find out vampires are real, eh? How long have I been here?"

Jackson clucked his tongue. "Two weeks."

"What?!" Ava made to jump out of the bed, but the wolf caught her and held her down. She hissed at him, batting his shoulder. "Let me up! Everybody is going to be worried sick!"

"I texted your work saying you had a family emergency. Your friend Melanie took a bit more convincing, but she thinks you're in Denver with your parents. If you think that I'm going to let you leave this house while Astrophel is out there, you are very wrong."

Ava crossed her arms over her chest.

"Are you going to, what, tie me up?"

He grinned. "Only if you want me to, kitten."

Ava blushed just thinking about that, trying not to imagine herself with her legs splayed and tied, helpless to his wants.

"Am I just supposed to stay here forever?" she said hotly, annoyed by how her body reacted to the image. Annoyed by his stupid, smug, handsome face. "I have a job, a life. I worked hard to get what I have; I'm not letting some vampire creep take it away from me."

"Then stay. You won't have a life if Astrophel gets to you," he said, his arms crossed over his chest.

Ava opened her mouth to snap back at him, but she held her breath instead. She had never been sick a day in her life, like all shifters. And this Astrophel guy had nearly killed her. Vampires might seem fantastical, but it was as good as any explanation... as long as she accepted that Jackson was genuinely here to help her.

"So, what's going on?" she asked to keep her mind from wandering.

Looking into his eyes was as comforting as it was disconcerting, and the only reason that Ava wasn't panicking was the fact that he soothed her somehow, even as he made her angry.

"Astrophel is a very powerful, very old vampire. He's king of a clan that resides in the mountains. Me and my people keep an eye on them, keep them from crossing the border."

"You aren't doing such a great job, are you?" Ava asked.

He gritted his teeth. "A shifter killed a vampire a while ago. According to our treaty, it means we have to hand a shifter over to him. An eye for an eye. He wants you."

A shiver ran down her spine. "Why me?"

Jackson shrugged. "Either it's random or he saw us in the woods and decided to fuck—sorry, mess—with me."

Her stomach twisted, the toast sitting uncomfortably in her gut. "He chose me... to get to you? Why?"

He shrugged again. "I killed his son."

Great. She was stuck in the middle of a blood feud. Her stomach churned worse and she had to wonder if it was wise to stay here with Jackson. "Why did you kill his son?"

"He killed my mother." A wry smile crossed his lips. "My parents were the alpha male and female of the Coalfell chapter—the front line against vampires. The Savage Brotherhood does more than control the local crime life, Kitten."

"You don't look like the leader of a superhero squad that protects the town. You look like the kind of guy who rides around, sits in a bar, drinks, takes a new girl home every night. Rinse and repeat."

He grinned. "All of those things are true."

Ava rolled her eyes, flushing under his gaze.

"I'm a biker—a pig, if that's what you think," Jackson said. "And yet I've kept girls like you alive for decades. The same kind of girls who cross the street if they see me walking toward them."

"Can you blame them?" Ava asked.

He gave her a dry grin. "You really think tattoos and leather tell you who I really am?"

"No. You've shown me who you are." She meant it to be a compliment. After all, he'd cared for her for two weeks while she was sick. His eyes flashed, though, and she could tell he was thinking about how their... play in the woods ended. She quickly continued. "What are we going to do about Astrophel?"

"*I'm* going to kill him," Jackson said.

"How?"

"It's none of your business," he said. "All you need to do is sit here until he's dead."

Ava opened her mouth to argue, but he stood up, staring down at her.

"I have to go call my sister, tell her you're awake. Astrophel's going to get impatient to have you sooner or later. We have to find the shifter who killed the vampire—if the vamps killed him, then Astrophel's claim on you is moot.

But you're still not fully recovered. Try to eat and get some rest."

Ava hesitated a moment before nodding. She did feel sleepy... Jackson stared at her for another long moment before nodding. He left without another word, leaving Ava wondering what that look was really about.

Chapter Four
Jackson

She was going to be alright. Jackson stood in Ava's doorway watching her sleep, just as he had been doing for the past two weeks. This time was different, though. She was still weak from the venom, but she was out of danger. The vamps hadn't tried anything so far. They weren't any closer to finding out who the shifter that killed the vampire in the woods was, though. It would be helpful if they had a copy of the pictures, but vampires weren't known for being helpful.

Her hair fell into her face as she shifted slightly. Jackson would have given anything to push that hair away. Looking at her sleeping peacefully, he wanted to kiss her eyelids and her lips. A moan left her lips and he wondered what she was dreaming about.

Jackson snorted. His cellphone buzzed and, with another snort, he snatched it out of his pocket. His wolf snarled when he saw who it was, and he quickly retreated to the downstairs.

"Typhoon," he greeted, keeping his voice flat. "I thought you'd be in contact earlier than this.'

"And I thought you'd get your head out of your ass on your own. I guess we were both wrong."

Typhoon was the alpha of the Savage Brotherhood. While Jackson was alpha of the local chapter, Typhoon ruled them all. It was an old organization, having served as a barrier between vampires and humans long enough that even some shifters had forgotten about their enemy's existence. Typhoon wasn't much older than Jackson himself, but he had a strength behind him that nobody could deny.

"I've received an official complaint from Astrophel," Typhoon continued. "You're blocking him from his chosen payment. What the hell are you thinking?"

"We don't know that the shifter who killed that vampire is even alive. If the vamps killed him, then he's their payment."

Typhoon snarled. Even over the line, it made Jackson's hair stand on end. His wolf snarled back, although he bowed his head in subservience on instinct. He'd seen Typhoon take out far older, stronger, and more experienced alphas for smaller betrayals than this, not to mention the sheer number of vampires he'd killed.

"Shadow told me you fucked her."

Jackson bit back another snarl. Why the hell would Val tell him *that*? He thought about Ava's face, the flush in her cheeks as they found completion together, the way her wild scent increased when she had welcomed him into her.

"I'm not letting the corpse get his hands on her."

"So, it has nothing to do with the shifter that killed the vamp." Typhoon's snarl became more pronounced. "Give her up, Tornado. We've been hit too hard the last few years to give up more for one girl, no matter how big her tits are."

Jackson opened his mouth to snarl at his alpha not to speak about Ava that way, but he stopped himself. Why was he feeling so protective of her? They hardly knew each other. Was she really worth losing his life over?

His wolf growled and snapped at his throat, furious at him for even thinking such a thing. Jackson pushed it down. Ava was under his protection because he didn't let anybody die at a vampire's hands for nothing. Especially not Astrophel, who only chose her because of the connection they had shared in the woods.

"I'm not handing her over," Jackson hurried to continue before Typhoon could snarl again, "until I have evidence that the shifter who killed that vampire wasn't already killed, I refuse to accept his claim to a life. We can't just let them walk all over us."

Typhoon snarled again, but it wasn't as angry this time. "Fine. I'll deal with Astrophel, you find this shifter and verify he's alive. And do it quick. I'm not a patient wolf."

Typhoon hung up. Jackson shoved his phone into his pocket and shook his head. Not a patient wolf? Understatement of the century.

***

Somewhere around dawn, Jackson was woken by the front door slamming. He was alert at once, a growl in his feet, as he sprang off the couch. Val shot him an annoyed look as she walked into the living room. Three tow-headed girls trailed after her. The oldest, Artemis, gave him a sleepy smile.

"Hi, Uncle Jackson."

Jackson smiled at his three nieces, though his heart plummeted at the sight of them. Something had to be wrong if Val dragged them out here. Was she that worried about Astrophel?

"You three go upstairs and get some more sleep," she told them, her voice the softest it ever was. The girls obediently trotted upstairs. Val waited until they were gone before she turned to him with a glare.

"What?" he asked.

"Your guys got busted, that's what," Val said, her voice dripping with irritation. "All because you haven't been around to keep them in line."

Jackson swore loudly, but Val smacked him hard. He winced, rubbing his arm. "What do you mean, they got busted?"

"I mean that the idiots decided to pull a job tonight. Eric was supposed to be driving, but he was drunk. They thought they'd be cute and not keep me in the loop. Blizzard has them now."

Jackson cursed. He hated when the sheriff got involved in his business, especially since Cunningham had been one of them once, before he'd yellowed out to become a military guy and a cop.

"Cunningham," he spat. He'd lost the right to his nickname when he left the gang. "I've told him not to mess with my guys."

"And he's told you to keep them straight. Blizzard doesn't care if you run your business, but he's not going to let you screw up and get him in trouble.

He's pissed. You'd better talk them out of jail, what with your kitten upstairs with a vampire on her tail."

Jackson glanced upwards. He didn't want to leave Ava alone, but she wouldn't be alone. Val and the girls were here. With a half-groan, half-sigh, he headed for the door.

"Be nice," he called over his shoulder, then was gone.

His mind was full of Ava as he drove to town. The heat in her eyes, her anger, the wild animal in her was what he wanted almost as much as he wanted a real smile from her. He had kissed her lips, felt both that smile and that animal. His wolf longed to be with her every moment of the day. Even now it whimpered at leaving her.

There was an explanation for that, but Jackson refused to even consider that she might be his mate.

It was impossible. He had heard about what it would be like to meet his mate—every shifter had. It was supposed to be magical, without any of the bickering. Jackson found it hard to believe that she could be his mate if they couldn't even get along enough to hold a conversation without fighting. Still, when he kissed her, his entire body felt like it was becoming part of a whole for the first time.

Just thinking about it pissed him off, mixed his feelings up so that by the time he got to the sheriff's office and local jail, his jaw was tight, his whole body wound up.

He was not in the mood for Cunningham's games and slammed the door open. He glanced around, catching sight of the older wolf. His eyes darkened as he stalked over.

Cunningham gazed at him coolly. "Masters."

"Cunningham."

The sheriff stared at him, holding the door open. Jackson held the man's eye as he stared across the desk. The two had formed an uneasy truce a long time ago, one that felt like it was on thin ice every time they saw each other. It was almost as delicate a balancing act as the treaty with the vampires.

"So, what'd you pick them up for?" Jackson said eventually. No use in pretending that he didn't know what he was there for.

"These morons tried to rob a jewelry store in Oak Town," the sheriff said, shaking his head. "No one was hurt, but the owner saw their faces. I'm charging all your guys. This was sloppy, Masters. You're getting cocky."

"No, Cunningham," Jackson growled. "We have a deal. You know that."

"Our deal is that your guys don't get caught, and I don't go looking for them. Your guys got caught tonight, Tornado. The Savage Brotherhood does their job, and I let you off the hook as long as you don't fuck up. They fucked up. They put themselves on the radar. I have no choice—"

"Listen, Cunningham," Jackson growled as he leaned on the desk. He loomed over the sheriff, but

Cunningham didn't so much as blink. "I need those guys out there. Astrophel has—"

"Astrophel's involved?" Cunningham's expression went from cool to focused. He got to his feet. "For how long?"

"Couple weeks," Jackson grunted. "Vamp was killed by a shifter, he's claimed a panther. I've been keeping her in the safe house while looking for proof that the shifter that killed the vamp is still alive."

Cunningham swore explosively. He ran a hand through his salt-and-pepper hair and glared at Jackson. "What the hell, Tornado? That's the sort of thing you tell me before it gets this far. And what the hell were you thinking, sending those idiots on a job while there's a vampire threat?"

"They acted without permission and will be punished for it. But I need them, idiots though they are, patrolling the borders. Nobody else can protect the humans and shifters from the vamps. Only my guys are equipped to handle it."

"Yeah, well, right now they're only equipped to sit in a cell in handcuffs," Cunningham snarled. "And I'm tempted to leave them that way for a few days."

Jackson shook his head. "Unacceptable. I need them now. Don't worry, they won't be getting anywhere near any jewelry stores. And by the time Val's through with them, they might not even have skin left."

Cunningham narrowed his eyes and snarled. Jackson's own wolf wanted to attack for the challenge, but he held himself back. It was that sort of impulsive action that nearly got him killed when Cunningham left the gang. He was smarter than that now.

"You really didn't give the orders?" the sheriff asked.

"No," said Jackson, his jaw tight. "Now we need to get out of here. I'll keep them in line."

Cunningham sighed, grabbing his keys from his drawer and standing up.

"I don't want a single vampire-related death in the city. If it happens, I'm taking your men in. You'd better hope they're not as useless as I think they are," the sheriff said as he stepped out of the room.

Jackson followed him back through a hall to the cell, where three men were sitting on a bench with their hands locked behind their backs. The men looked up at Jackson with bashful looks as the sheriff unlocked the cell. Jackson glared at the three of them, and each of them flinched.

"Basil, Tony, Eric, you're free to go," Cunningham said, unlocking them one at a time. "Stay out of my sight for a few weeks."

"Yes, sir," said Basil, the youngest of them, a lion shifter that Jackson had only taken on in his gang because of his strength as an animal.

The three of them filed out after Jackson, who didn't speak to any of them. He gestured at the truck he'd driven there, and they silently climbed into the bed. He didn't want to talk to any of them, nor look at their faces.

"Jackson," the sheriff called after him before Jackson got back into the truck.

"What is it?"

"Like I said, one vamp attack, I'm bringing your guys in. Doesn't look to me like they're doing any good."

"We'll stop Astrophel," Jackson said harshly as he started the truck.

He took off, driving back to the bar where he'd left his motorcycle. It was cold outside, but he wanted it back, wanted to ride it to the safe house and feel the wind pressing against him, pressing his thoughts out of his mind.

Jackson nodded at Les as they made their way behind the counter to the small room at the back of the bar. He almost expected to see Val there, but she wasn't to be seen. He remembered her taking the girls out to the safehouse. She wouldn't leave them there with Ava as a babysitter—Val trusted very few people with her babies.

"Tornado—" Eric started

Jackson whirled, a snarl in his throat. The three men backed up and dropped their heads. His fists clenched, and he resisted the urge to beat some sense into them.

"You three are on forest patrol until further notice. Go up to the ranger shack."

The three of them groaned, but at the look on his face, they fell silent again.

"Do you think this is a fucking game?" he seethed at them. "We have a sacred duty to protect those who cannot protect themselves. We have fun, but we don't let it interfere with what we have to do. Now get the hell out of here before I decide to rip out your throats. None of you sleep until this is over. If a vamp attack happens in your sector, I'm either going to put you in a cell or in the ground. Got it?"

Basil swallowed hard. "Y—yes, sir."

The others nodded silently. Jackson glared at the three of them for a moment longer before he gestured for them to leave. They scrambled out quickly, heading for their bikes at once.

Jackson stopped at the bar to get a bracing drink to calm his nerves. Les gave him a look he knew all too well.

"What?" he snapped at the bartender.

Les smirked. "This girl's gotten under your skin, hasn't she? You're just as surly and distracted as your dad was when he met your mom. They were a real couple. If they weren't so in love, they'd have killed each other before you had the chance to be born."

The tension in Jackson's shoulders eased as he was reminded of his parents. He hesitated a moment, wondering if he could confide in Les, but decided against it. He downed his drink and threw a handful of bills on the counter.

"See you around," he grunted and went for his bike.

It was cold, but Jackson didn't care—the leather jacket he was wearing kept him insulated as he flew down the street, getting on the highway to head back to the safe house. He wondered if Ava was up and, if so, what she thought about the fact that he had just disappeared on her.

He wasn't comforted by the knowledge that Val would be there. Now that he thought about it, actually, leaving Ava with his sister could turn out to be a big mistake. Val wasn't one for niceties. He pushed the bike hard, wanting to get back to her as quickly as possible.

Chapter Five
Ava

When Ava woke the next morning, she heard... the laughter of children? That couldn't be right. Frowning, she quickly dressed and headed downstairs. Her headache was gone, although her legs were a bit weak. And there was a gaping hole in her chest where her panther should be. She swallowed, unnerved, but determined that she'd ask Jackson.

She had just reached the bottom of the stairs when a girl, no more than six, streaked past, giggling like a maniac. An older girl chased after her, brandishing hands gooey with cookie dough.

"Ah...." Ava stared after them for a moment.

"You're finally awake."

Ava turned to the gruff female voice to find a woman glaring at her. She wore a long-sleeved shirt, but tattoos peaked up from her neckline. Heavy braids hung from one side of her head while the other was shaved. The look in her eyes was sheer hatred.

"Who are you?" Ava demanded, not one to be intimidated even though her panther hissed at the other woman.

"Name's Shadow. I'm Tornado's sister. He'll be back soon." Shadow wrinkled her nose as she gazed at Ava for a long moment, then the harsh glare on her face softened. "Now I know why Jackson is so protective of you."

Ava stared at her for a moment. There was a bang and a shriek from another room, and a three-year-old came running into the room, her face full of fury. "Sekhmet broke my pony!"

"Then you'd better go make her fix it." Shadow smiled at the little girl. "Remember, us girls take care of ourselves."

The girl bunched up her fists and nodded like she had been assigned a suicide mission and took off again. Ava stared after her with a dropped jaw, until Shadow cleared her throat and gestured for her to follow.

"Um... what's that about?"

"I like my girls to fight their own fights."

"But shouldn't you—" Ava cut off at the glare Shadow gave her. Of course, if she was a gangster, and their uncle was a gangster, and with vampires out there... those girls were going to have to grow up tough as nails. She didn't wipe the disapproving frown from her face, though. "What were you saying about why Jackson's protective of me?"

"He knocked you up."

Ava stopped dead. Her jaw hung loose and her eyes widened as she stared at Shadow, who stopped to give her an irritated look.

"He did not!"

The other woman pointed to her belly. "There's a baby growing inside of you. Us females are more sensitive to the changes that happen in pregnancy than males are. You've got a pup inside of you. I can smell the wolf. You're pregnant, sweetheart."

Ava shook her head. "That's—that's impossible!"

It wasn't though. She had allowed Jackson to finish inside of her the night they had met, had encouraged it when she'd wrapped her legs around his waist. But it had only been two weeks ago, and there was no way to tell that she was pregnant already.

"I'm not pregnant," she said.

"Keep telling yourself that, cupcake," Shadow replied smoothly. "While the girls are occupied, you and I need to talk about this. Now come on or I'll drag you."

Ava had no doubt that Shadow would, in fact, drag her out of there. Stunned and silent, she followed after the other woman. Once they passed into the kitchen, which smelled like freshly baked cookies, Shadow closed the door and turned to her. Her arms folded over her chest and she gave Ava a stern look.

"You should have used a condom."

Ava's cheeks flushed, and she dropped her head.

"But since you didn't... you've got to decide what you're going to do."

"What... what do you mean?"

Shadow rolled her eyes. "You know what I mean. You got any family? A solid place to live? Stable job?"

Ava's mind flashed over the questions. She was on good terms with her parents, but her place here was only big enough for one, and the waitress job... well, she hated it. It was the worst thing she'd ever had to do, and she had been certain that she'd just switch it out for a more fun job when the time came.

If she was pregnant, though... she'd have to take a new job right away. Or would she stay waitressing until she could go on maternity leave? She swallowed hard as she considered it.

"Uh..."

Shadow's face softened further. "Look, I'm a single mom myself. I know how hard it is to make this decision. And you've got to consider that the corpses have claimed you. There's no way to prove they claimed you before you got preggers, and so it's part of the claim. For all intents and purposes, you're one individual when it comes to the claim, even if you live long enough to give birth."

Ava's hands drifted to her stomach. A fire lit in her chest and she snarled. "I'll kill you if you try to hurt my baby!"

Shadow's eyes widened slightly, then she nodded. "Okay. I guess you've made that choice... Now, what are you going to tell Jackson?"

"I don't see how it's any of your—"

"He's my brother. I know him." Shadow pulled a sheet of cookies from the oven and put in the second batch. It seemed odd to see such a badass woman do something so... domestic. When she glanced at Ava again, there was deep pity in her eyes. "He's attached. Whether to you or because he subconsciously realizes you're carrying his baby, I don't know. But he'll kill for you. He'll die for you. And ultimately? He'll stand down as Alpha of our chapter for you."

Ava couldn't reply to that. It couldn't be true... could it? Her stomach twisted, and she couldn't hold Shadow's gaze. Jackson hardly knew her. She hardly knew him. He wouldn't be willing to give her everything... would he?

"I don't know why this is such a concern to you," Ava grumbled, her shoulders tightening.

"Because if we lose him as Alpha, we're vulnerable. It will take time to get a new leader selected, and in that time, things will break down. Vampires will break through. So, can you have a mate that's the alpha of a gang? Cause if you can't..." Shadow shrugged. "Then, leave him alone."

Ava's nostrils flared. Her hands clenched, angered by the cold way Shadow said that, as though she had the right to dictate Ava's relationship with Jackson. Which didn't mean she had one, but if she did, then Shadow had no right to start telling her what to do.

"I'll do what I want, thank you very much. And if you're so worried, then maybe—"

Shadow snarled, but before things could escalate further, there was a shriek, and somebody started to cry. Shadow shot Ava a filthy look and left the kitchen. Ava's hands shook, unnerved by this whole thing.

Pregnant.

What the fuck was she going to do?

***

Ava returned to her room shortly after she ate, overwhelmed by the 'p-word' hanging over her head. When Jackson arrived, Shadow loaded up her three daughters in a minivan that didn't suit her at all and drove off without a word. Once she heard Jackson moving around downstairs, Ava padded down to greet him.

She found him combing his hair with his fingers, grimacing in the mirror when he saw that it wouldn't lay down. Ava had to smile when she saw him, his slight frown, the look of frustration on his face. It was an endearing look on such a tough man—a man who presented himself as anything other than soft or concerned about how he came off.

He jumped when she cleared her throat, then turned to her with a slight smile. "Ava. Val told me that you rested all day? That's good. You still need to build your strength."

Had Shadow also told him about her pregnancy?

No. She'd been very clear that this was Ava's choice—or mistake—to make. A tremor ran through her hands as she stared off to one side, not meeting Jackson's gaze. Rested? She felt anything but. She needed to move, to breathe again.

"I want to go for a walk." He started to shake his head, but stopped when she met his eyes. "Please, Jackson."

The wolf froze. He looked torn for a moment, but then something passed over his face and he nodded. "Alright. But I have to go with you."

She rolled her eyes. "Of course, you do. Can't have a damn second of privacy around here."

Jackson sighed. He ran a hand through his hair, undoing his efforts to make it lay flat. "I don't want to fight with you today. I'm tired of it. Think you can play nice?"

"Depends on whether or not you're an asshole."

He smiled at her then. "I'll try not to be an asshole."

Her stomach fluttered at that, her heart feeling a little lighter. A smile started to spread over her face, but she stopped it quickly. He was the leader of a dangerous gang. Yeah, they fought vampires, but that wasn't all that they did. And Shadow had been very clear. If Ava wanted Jackson, she'd have to accept the whole gang.

That was something she just couldn't do.

For a moment, Ava wondered if she should just call off the walk. But her legs burned with the desire to move. She wanted to feel the cool wind on her body after so many days cooped in the house. Ava wanted to see the world around her, anything outside of the walls she had been trapped inside for weeks. And maybe getting out and under the stars would awaken her panther again.

"Are you ready?" he asked her.

Ava nodded. She followed him outside, taking a deep breath of the fresh air. They started walking through the trees, following no real path but the places where footsteps had tread on and crushed new spring grass. The silence between them was comfortable—too comfortable.

"So. You killed Astrophel's son because he killed your mother. And that's why he's after me?"

Jackson glanced at her with a frown but nodded. "It would seem to be so. My parents were the founding members of this chapter. The Savage Brotherhood is old, very old, but we've only been in Coalfell for, oh... thirty years. It used to be that the vampires would walk among the humans, taking them as they wanted. Astrophel's son was the sheriff and Astrophel was the mayor. Nobody could touch them. My parents drove them out, but... paid the ultimate price for it. After they died, Val and I decided to lead the chapter. I became the alpha and she, my enforcer."

"And this is very important to you, isn't it? Being a Savage Brother and fighting the vampires."

Jackson gave her a crooked smile and laughed. "More important than anything else."

Ava looked away. Shadow's words that he'd step down as alpha for her and the baby rang in her ears. Could she really ask him to stop defending people for her? And could she turn a blind eye to the drugs, the robberies...?

"What about you?" he asked, his gaze still intent on her. "What's your tragic backstory?"

Ava shrugged. "I grew up with shifter parents. I always knew what I was. I went to school, went to college—my degree didn't work out, and now I work at a coffee shop. There's not much to me."

"I don't believe that."

"What else is there?"

"Well... why Coalfell? Out of all the places to go, why here?"

Ava shrugged again. "I was... trying to find a calmer life. Striking out on my own. Being my own panther..."

Her hand touched her chest, where her panther should be. For a wild moment, she wanted to tell him about this dangerous absence, but swallowed it down. She didn't know him, not really, and she couldn't reveal such a vulnerable piece of information. Quickly, she turned the conversation back to him.

"What are you going to do about Astrophel?"

Jackson frowned. "At the moment, I'm trying to prove that he has no right to you. It's more than likely that he killed the shifter that was on his territory. I hate waiting around, but it's all I can do right now."

Ava shivered. "And if you don't find proof?"

"Val's on the hunt for the corpse. When she finds him..."

Another shiver, stronger this time. "When she finds him?"

"I'll kill him."

Ava turned to him. The sunlight was soft and dusky as it filtered through the branches, but it didn't soften the bloodlust in his eyes. A thrill of fear went down her spine, and she shook her head hard.

"You can't! If you do that, then the vampires will be able to choose another shifter. What if they choose you?"

Jackson arched a brow. "They wouldn't take on the brotherhood like that."

"Unless it's their plan already. Astrophel targeted me. It's one hell of a coincidence if he chose me before we... ran in the woods together. He's wanting to provoke you to do something stupid. So, you can't, okay? You can't be stupid."

"I can do whatever I want. And I want to kill him."

Ava grabbed him by the shoulders and shook him, frustration welling in her. "No!"

"Are you always like this?" he asked her, a grin spreading across his face. "Or is it just with me?"

"Like what?" she asked.

"Stubborn. Completely impossible."

"As if you're not the same way."

Jackson snorted softly. "You have a point there."

"Good to know."

For a moment, they were quiet, their eyes locked together as they stood there. Ava felt a stirring in her body, heat flashing under her skin. She swallowed dryly as her gaze flickered to his mouth. He started in, eyes hungry, but she turned her face away before he could kiss her.

Jackson froze. Then he stepped back, running a hand through his hair again.

It took great effort, but she once more looked him in the eye. "I am not going to be a gangster's side piece."

Jackson stepped back. For a moment, disappointment flashed in his face, but the look was replaced quickly by a hard shell, as though nothing had passed between them. He shrugged. "Okay. Whatever you want, Kitten. We should get back to the house, though. There aren't any charms out here against the vampires."

She nodded stiffly. The walk back was brisker than it had been leaving, and all too soon Ava was back in the house. Her stomach grumbled but she had no appetite, so she went back upstairs. For some stupid reason, her eyes started to burn, and she rubbed the back of her hand over them. There was no reason to be so sad... she had done what was best.

He was a gangster. A dangerous man. Yes, he had cared for her when she was sick. He had looked after her. He was protecting her. But he was a gangster. He had a blood feud with vampires—a feud she had been caught up in just because she slept with him.

And now she had far more than herself to worry about. Her hand rested on her belly as she made her choice.

Jackson would never know about this baby.

Chapter Six
Jackson

The sound of multiple motorcycle engines had Jackson tensing. This late at night, any members of the gang headed out this way ought to have phoned first. He moved to the window and peered through the night. Soon, headlights came into view. Two of them. He recognized Val's shadow as she climbed off her bike and shook out her braids. The other was big, hulking.

Jackson moved to the porch. His wolf snarled, though he kept his own expression calm.

"Tornado," the stranger called in greeting.

Jackson took a moment to place the voice. "Thunder."

He was the alpha of the Ivywood chapter. Jackson tensed. If he was here, that meant that Typhoon was furious, and was checking up on him. Jackson growled as the two approached, though he kept his gaze on his sister.

"Didn't expect you to stab me in the back," he snarled.

Val rolled her eyes. "If I was going to stab you in the back, brother, you'd never know it was me. Thunder's got words for you."

"Can I come—"

"No." Jackson folded his arms. "You can't. Say what you've got to say and then leave my territory."

Thunder smirked a moment. "Touchy. We found your boy. The shifter that killed the vampire. He's dead. Clear signs of vamp-inflicted wounds."

Jackson's heart rose at once. He dropped his arms and stepped forward, eyes alight. "Then they have no right to Ava. I was right! That corpse can take his claim and shove it—"

"We will have to meet with him. Show him proof he has no claim." Thunder sounded bored. "And then you have to report to Typhoon. He's not gonna let you off easy, even if you were right. What's this girl done to you, man? You're like a little puppy on a string."

"Shut up," Val snapped. "What goes on over here is none of your concern. Typhoon never should have sent you. We're more than capable of dealing with this on our own."

Jackson smiled at his sister, grateful for her support. She narrowed her eyes at him in clear warning. If he screwed this up, there'd be no mercy from her. He nodded briefly, then stepped back inside.

"I assume the meeting's already been arranged?"

"We've got two hours to get to Astrophel," she confirmed. "You remember that old warehouse out on Pine? It used to be a canning place?"

"Yes," said Jackson. "He's there?"

Val nodded. "Go get the girl. We'll have to make him take the mark off her, or else she'll be stuck here forever."

Jackson hesitated. Taking Ava to the vampire who wanted to kill her was a bad idea. And yet, if they didn't have the mark removed, then she'd be vulnerable. The vampires would think they had claim to her. They wouldn't stop coming for her. So, with a sigh, he headed back inside.

Surprised, he came face-to-face with Ava as soon as he rounded the corner. Her eyes were bright, and her hands twisted.

"Did I hear right?"

He nodded. Part of him wondered if Ava would do something stupid... If their places were reversed, he'd feel like he deserved some vengeance on Astrophel. Ava didn't seem to be that kind of person, though. She seemed like the kind to forgive and forget... at least, he hoped she was.

"We're going to meet Astrophel. We've got proof he has no right to claim you and—"

"I'm going with you."

Jackson nodded reluctantly. "We're going to need you there so Astrophel can remove the mark he made on you."

She nodded. There was fear in her eyes, but anticipation and excitement, too. Was she really so eager to be rid of him that she'd face down a vampire? What was he thinking—of course, she was. Her words from earlier made his jaw clench. *I won't be a gangster's side piece.*

He wanted to tell her that it wasn't what he wanted from her, but, honestly, how could he say something like that? Whatever connection they had, it wasn't the kind to last. They were thrown together by circumstances, nothing more.

"Jackson..." For the first time, a look of vulnerability shone from her eyes.

"What is it?"

"I can't shift," said Ava, her voice cracking. "I tried. I can't even feel my panther... it's just... blank."

His brow furrowed in concern. He took her hand and led her deeper into the house, where Val and Thunder wouldn't be able to overhear their conversation. They sat on the couch and Ava twisted her hands. Was this why she had been pushing him away? Because she was afraid something was wrong with her?

He touched her chin, gently guiding her gaze to his. "It's the venom. Sometimes this happens. It's not permanent, but we can't take you in there if you can't defend yourself."

"I don't feel sick," Ava said.

He took a deep breath, glancing at her lips, then back up at her face. There was one sure-fire way to bring a faded animal back to the forefront. It was hiding because it didn't feel safe. Because of the venom, threatening to turn it rabid. But there was nothing left in her system, and it needed to emerge.

"Can I try something?" he asked.

"What?" Ava asked him, her voice trembling slightly.

"I think if I kiss you—"

Ava shook her head but didn't look away from his eyes. "What—what does that have to do with anything?"

Jackson wasn't sure how to answer that. "Your panther, she's scared. She needs to know that it's safe to come out. She trusts me. We've already had sex, she knows that I'm the wolf she can play with. It will let her feel safe , so she can come forward."

Her hands continued to twist. She glanced away, and then back at him. He understood her desperation.

"I've gone through this myself," he added softly. "I know it feels like you're barely half a person. I promise this will help. And all it has to be is one kiss."

Her hands stopped fidgeting. Finally, her eyes met his fully and she nodded. Her whole body was stiff and tense. He frowned, but didn't comment on it. She had every right to be tense. Slowly, he moved closer.

He touched her cheek again, pulling her face forward for a soft kiss. Ava gasped as he sucked on her lips, slipping his tongue into her mouth. Her taste was enough to drive him to distraction. Heat flared under his skin as he moved closer; he pulled her into his lap. She began to respond as he tasted her, opening her mouth to him, letting him in. His wolf growled with pleasure. He thought he heard a purr in response.

"How's that?" he asked against her lips.

Ava's eyes closed. Her whole lush body pressed against him, making him want more. He wanted to lay her down and meld with her, so close that they were one body. He wanted to swear to be hers for the rest of eternity. He wanted...

Her mouth found his again. This time she took charge, delving deep. Her arms wrapped around his neck as he pressed against her, hungry, his whole body trembling against hers. Desire coursed through his veins and he heard a panther's snarl, evoking a howl from his wolf. He could feel her getting closer, eager to join the fun. Ava whimpered as their mouths moved together.

Jackson pulled away, studying her face. His wolf snarled at him for stopping, but he knew he had to. Desire pulsed under his skin. But she didn't want this.

"Try to shift," he said to her. "I can feel her inside of you. Your panther. Can you feel her?"

The next thing he knew, the black panther was in his lap. She sprang from him, wriggling out of her clothes before she started to race around the room. She leapt onto the walls, springing off with such strength and grace, he was left breathless. When she landed, her yellow eyes gleamed, and her tail flicked back and forth. She leapt forward at him, knocking him to the ground on his back, her massive paws pinning his shoulders.

Ava growled at him playfully. He couldn't stop himself from grinning back at her.

"See? It worked."

She shifted back to human form, still on top of him. Her hands pressed against his chest and from this angle, he could see every inch of her bared, curvy form. "I want this vampire dead. I want to get out of here."

He opened his mouth to say that they couldn't kill Astrophel, but she was already gone. Jackson watched her dress, hating that such a body had to be covered, then got to his feet.

The others waited outside, arms crossed, as they came out. Ava glanced warily at Thunder before turning to Jackson.

"Where's the car?"

Jackson shook his head. "We'll take my bike."

"Your motorcycle?"

"Yeah. You scared?" he asked her teasingly. She crossed her arms over her chest, tilting her chin upward and giving him a defiant look.

"No," she said. "I've just never ridden one before."

"I'm sure you're a natural," Jackson said. "I seem to remember that you're very good at riding."

She blushed, and he grinned at her, enjoying the heated look on her face. Some of the stress of the situation eased as he walked with her to his bike. Thunder watched them openly, a curious expression on his face. Val just scowled and looked in the opposite direction.

When he climbed on, though, Ava hesitated.

"Chicken."

"I'm not a chicken. I eat chicken."

Jackson shrugged. "You are what you eat."

She laughed, the sound soft and sweet, rare coming from her. Then she climbed on behind him, wrapping her body around his, her chest pressed against his back as he started the bike. The feeling of her lush body pressed against his was distracting, and all Jackson wanted was to turn around and kiss her, pull her inside, forget about Astrophel, and take her to bed, where they belonged.

Instead, he pulled away from the house, heading toward the warehouse. Val rode at his right side, Thunder at his left. The other alpha kept pushing his bike forward, threatening to outpace him. Jackson ignored the obvious attempts to goad him. Thunder just liked to cause a scene.

Instead, he focused on Ava. Her arms wrapped around his waist, her face pressed close. Her heat warmed him as they rode through the cool wind. When this was over... it was going to be over between them. She'd go about her life, and he'd return to his.

It was probably for the best. This way, Astrophel would have no reason to target her again.

Still, the thoughts played about his head. The only way to be sure Astrophel never came after her was to kill him. Jackson knew that the best way to go about killing the vampire was to keep him out until the sun came up. Astrophel would burn away into nothing, and the vamps would have no proof that he had been killed by a shifter. And technically he wouldn't have been... but Jackson also knew Astrophel would never fall for that. He was much too old and smart.

The warehouse was huge and forbidding. Jackson brought the bike to a standstill, then helped Ava off before he climbed off himself. Val and Thunder followed suit. Val's nose twitched as she tested the air. Jackson caught a faint whiff of sweetness, but that was all he could tell from the vampires. Val's senses were much more finely tuned.

"There are at least three of them," she muttered. "Astrophel's here."

"Right, then." Jackson rolled his shoulders. "Stay close. Thunder, you're here to present evidence, but this is my gig. Stay out of it unless I ask you to speak."

He snorted, but nodded. Jackson finally turned to Ava. Uncertainty crossed her face, but it was gone before he could question if she was alright. A determined scowl answered him, and she nodded. Together, the four of them walked into the warehouse.

Astrophel was already waiting with two of his more muscled goons. They sneered at the shifters. Jackson's wolf growled.

"So, you've brought me my claim," Astrophel said in a bored tone. "I was beginning to lose patience."

"You have no claim," Jackson growled. "You already took your restitution for the vampire killed. The shifter that killed your man is dead by vampire wounds."

Astrophel's lip curled back. "Is that so?"

"It is," Thunder said. He stepped forward.

Jackson couldn't stop himself from snarling. "We brought proof."

Thunder tossed a cellphone to the vampires. Astrophel caught it with ease and flicked through the images. A look of disappointment came across his face, and he shook his head.

"I see. Such a simple mission and he still managed to fail."

The hairs on Jackson's neck rose. "What are you talking about?"

"If you are half as clever as you think, you will be able to figure it out." Astrophel made a small gesture with his hand. His nostrils flared as he turned to look at Ava. Jackson felt her shudder as the vampire smiled. "But no distractions. My claim is still here. Hello, my dear... You are stronger than I thought. Perhaps you are all that will be required."

Jackson started forward. "Listen, you corpse—"

Before he could get out another word, the doors flung open. A dozen vampires poured in, hands outstretched like claws, fangs bared and fearsome howls in the air.

Jackson shifted at once. Ava shrieked, but when he glanced over his shoulder, she had shifted to her black panther. Val growled in her Leopard form, and beside her, Thunder charged the vampires coming at them.

They were on neutral territory. This attack was more than enough justification to go after Astrophel. Jackson whirled about, launching himself towards the vampire king.

Before he could reach him, though, a vampire came out of nowhere. It rammed into Jackson's side, throwing him off course. Jackson skidded several feet, snarling and biting at the vampire.

It bared its teeth in a laugh. Strong arms wrapped around his chest. Jackson threw himself forward, teeth clamping over the vampire's lower jaw to prevent it from biting him. The vampire shrieked. Jackson used his momentum to fling the vamp onto its back, and then shook him from side to side. Bone snapped, and the vampire's head came cleanly off.

Jackson barked in triumph and turned once more, but Astrophel was nowhere to be seen. Suddenly, a scream rose up behind him. He whirled, eyes widening as he saw Ava grabbed by the throat and hoisted into the air. He threw himself forward, running hard, but the vampire flew high into the air, out of his reach. Val came out of nowhere. She jumped on his back and sprang into the air, using him as leverage.

Her paws swiped just under Ava's feet before she fell back to the ground.

Astrophel laughed as Ava screamed again. "It is fitting, Jackson Masters, that your blood will be what resurrects my son. Kill them all," he ordered, and then was gone.

Jackson let out a mournful howl. But then the rest of the vampires were closing in on him. The last he saw of Ava, she was clinging desperately to Astrophel's arm, calling his name.

Chapter Seven
Ava

The ground flashed below in a dizzying array of color. Wind rushed in her ears. All Ava could do was hold onto the vampire as they flew through the air. She couldn't even scream. Her panther had retreated the moment he touched her, leaving her in her human form. Now he had both arms around her waist. Her own hold was around his neck, desperate not to fall to her death.

Ava shut her eyes so that she wouldn't have to see herself flying, and she only hoped that he wouldn't decide to drop her before they got to the caves. At one point a low chuckle grated on her ears, but Astrophel didn't try to speak. Flashes of light passed under them, then they were but a shadow rippling in the moonlight.

Ava wasn't sure how long they were in the air; it felt like hours. Eventually, the vampire dove downward. The rush of air pulled at her skin as they plummeted. She opened her mouth to scream, but her breath was ripped from her throat. Just before they were speared on the trees, Astrophel slowed. He flipped them over, so that they landed lightly on their feet.

Ava tore herself away from the vampire at once. Her knees buckled, and she fell. Rocks bit into her palms, but she was too thankful to be on the ground once more to care.

"Get up." Astrophel's voice held a command.

Her panther retreated a little further, but Ava didn't let it disappear. Anger pooled in her chest, coaxing her panther to the surface. She let out a roar and lunged at him, but he caught her by the throat once more and lifted her body from the ground. Her weight pulled down until it felt like her neck would snap.

When he set her down again, she stumbled but stayed where she was.

Wind brushed against her back and goosebumps rose along her arms as she realized she was utterly naked, having lost her clothes when she shifted the first time. Bile rose in her throat and she stumbled away from the vampire.

"If you are a good, obedient girl, I will not molest you," he told her, voice cold as the air around them. "I have no taste for bestiality."

He cocked his head, nodded when he saw she was sufficiently subdued, and removed his jacket to hand to her. It was far too small on her large frame, but she could at least gain some sense of modesty with it. The vampire gripped her shoulder and spun her around. He shoved, and she walked over an uneven ground. The dark mouth of a cave loomed before them, but Astrophel didn't let Ava hesitate as he shoved her inside.

The darkness was almost too deep for her, but as her panther slowly returned to the surface, her eyes adjusted. Astrophel propelled her toward a large metal cage. The thick bars of steel were somehow drilled right into the stone of the floor below. Above, it twisted over itself and ended in spikes that pointed down.

The scent of blood was strong in the cave, and bits of fur clinging to those spikes told Ava exactly what it was from.

Ava took a deep breath as Astrophel flung her into the cage and locked it. She turned, her hands clenched. As much as she was glad to be alive right now, she didn't want to end up waiting around in terror for him to come finish the job.

"What are you going to do with me?"

Astrophel leaned against the metal bars. "What do you know about vampires, *Kitten*?"

Her panther snarled in protest of the vampire using Jackson's pet name for her. She snarled, too, but his cold, dead eyes stopped her from protesting. Her heart pounded.

"Not much," she admitted. "Until you attacked me, I didn't know vampires existed."

Astrophel nodded, as though in approval. "The treaty has worked, then. Even shifters are unaware of us... Once the Savage Brotherhood is gone, the world will be ours."

"That's great." Ava tried to give her voice more bravado than she felt. "But that doesn't say what you're going to do with me. You said that Jackson's blood was going to raise your son..."

Astrophel smiled this time. "He will figure out where you are, and he will come for you. Shifters on vampire territory are fair game. I will drain his blood, and, with it, perform the ritual of the Blood Moon to raise my son back. Jackson stole him from me. I will have him back... after I take everything from that dog."

Ava's heart hammered. He meant to kill Jackson to resurrect his son? It was impossible... right? Somehow, though, she knew she had to keep Astrophel from knowing how much she cared. "So, you're going to kill me."

"No, I don't think I will. Not until your mate gets here."

"He's not my mate."

Astrophel only smiled.

Her mind whirled. A thousand questions flitted through it, but she couldn't land on any of them. The vampire still stared at her, that cruel smile on his face. Eventually, she had to back further away from him, closer to the back wall of the cage.

"Stay put." Astrophel chuckled as he moved back to the mouth of the cage. "I have preparations to make."

He disappeared, letting her breathe again. The first thing she did was test the bars, to see if they had any give. The lock rattled, but that was it. Scratches lined the floor around the cage. How many others had been here, had wondered desperately how to get out?

Eventually, Ava was too exhausted to keep trying. She curled on the floor, the stinking vampire scent from Astrophel's jacket clogging her nose. It was pitiful protection. Even now when there were no prying eyes, she felt exposed.

Tears started to burn her eyes. *I will not cry.*

She closed her eyes. Desperate, she searched for some thought, some hope. Something that would alleviate the ache in her chest, the fear choking her. An image of Jackson's face flashed through her mind. The smile he gave her in the bar, the hard planes of his body as he undressed.

Hunger flared in his eyes as he kissed her, long and deep. She could almost taste him now. His hands explored her body, hot, demanding against her skin. She whimpered, helpless under his touch. She had never felt anything so... explosive before. It was like fireworks going off under her skin, making heat flare in her core. The forest disappeared around her until it was just the two of them and nothing more.

His hands ran up her thighs, tracing a delicate pattern that had her aching for more. She squirmed under his touch, his mouth still on hers. He pulled back slightly to give her that crooked grin, eyes glowing with lust as he looked down her body. Ava couldn't remember the last time anybody had looked at her that way.

His fingers found their way to her clit and she gasped, arching herself to him. Her head fell back. Her wolf gave a deep chuckle as he kneeled back and gripped her thighs tightly. With one movement, he opened them like a flower. His eyes riveted on the juncture of her legs. Ava could smell her own arousal.

She flushed pink all over and tried to close them, embarrassed by her arousal. The wolf held her firmly splayed open, though, and shot her a quizzical look.

"What's the matter, Kitten? Afraid of water?"

Now in the cave, Ava giggled at the memory. It was just the sort of thing Jackson would say! At the time, though, she had been even more mortified...

"I'll lick you dry, then," he murmured, lowering his face.

Ava opened her mouth, whether to protest or encourage she didn't know. It was lost as he began to do exactly as he promised. He licked her, teasing her, not quite going to her clit. Ava found her hips lifting in desperation against his face, wanting more. His hands were so tight on her thighs she felt like she might spin off into an endless nothingness if he released her.

"You didn't like me when you first met me in the bar," Jackson said, licking her again, nuzzling both her thighs. "Did you?"

"No," she breathed, letting out a soft moan when he wrapped his lips around her clit and started to suck on it, flicking it with his tongue.

"I think you like me now," he said. "At least a little bit."

"Please," she said softly, the word pushing out of her throat accidentally when he lifted his mouth to speak again.

He chuckled but did as she wanted. He devoured her, making the heat inside of her reach such a breaking point she was afraid she might burst into flames. One hand tangled into his hair, pressing against his face as he slipped his tongue inside of her to taste her from the source.

Ava trembled beneath him. His fingers replaced his tongue, then, sliding inside of her, beginning to curl upward in a way that hit the perfect spot inside of her body. She squirmed, whimpering, rocking her hips as he licked and sucked on her throbbing clit. She was on the edge, about to finish when he pulled away from her.

"What the hell?" was the first thing that burst from her.

If Jackson was here with her now, maybe she wouldn't be so cold...

"You're not going to come until I'm inside of you," he said gruffly. "Do you understand?"

Ava's nostrils flared. She didn't let anybody tell her what to do. Looking into the wolf's eyes, she reached between her legs, moaning when she found her clit.

"God!" the wolf breathed deeply as he grasped himself. "Don't do that! I almost lost it right there. You're so goddamn sexy."

She rubbed harder, enjoying the way his eyes hooded as he watched her. Then he had her by the thighs again. With one hand he pinned her hand over her head, the other guiding himself into her. Ava's head flung back, crying out as bursts of pleasure filled her. She moved her hips, arching them to take him as deep as she could. He started to rock in and out of her, moving slowly against her body in long strokes, pulling almost all the way out before he filled her again and again.

"Does that feel good, kitten?" he asked.

"Mhm," she breathed, her eyes rolling back as he found that spot again, pressing against it with deep, hard thrusts.

Ava's hips were already going wild, moving on their own accord in a natural rhythm with his own. She moaned loudly the second he reached down to rub her clit with two fingers, straddling it and stroking the sensitive areas surrounding. It was like he already knew what her body wanted, what she needed, and was doing almost more than she could bear.

"Are you ready?" he purred.

Ava curled with her back against the bars. She ached to have him in her arms right now, to kiss her, to tell her everything was going to be alright. But it wasn't. Even if they got out of this, she saw now more than ever why Shadow was so concerned about him leaving—if he stepped down as Alpha, how many would be taken by vampires in the chaos that followed?

"Mm," she breathed.

He took her mouth in a kiss as he found her opening again, pressing inside with a hard stroke. His hips started moving quickly, just the way she wanted him to.

Ava gave one last desperate breath before her body shuddered, her hips out of control. He kept going, his teeth bared in his concentration, before his body froze, grinding inside of her. He started to pull out, but Ava found herself wrapping her legs around his hips, wanting desperately to feel him finishing inside of her. He did so then, coming deep inside of her, rocking in and out until he was finished. He pulled away, then, and Ava panted in the aftershocks of pleasure that washed over her.

"That good for you?" he asked, stroking her face.

Ava nodded.

The wolf stretched and sighed. "Ah, yes. I needed that. Thanks, Kitten. Too bad it's over."

No. She wouldn't go past that.

His eyes burned with hunger as he kissed her. The forest melted away, until it was just the two of them and the heat they built between their bodies.

Reliving that moment over and over again, Ava eventually fell asleep.

***

She woke to a pale light coming from the mouth of the cave. Astrophel moved about near the back, chanting as he lit candles and drew on the floor with chalk. A body lay nearby.

Ava cried out in horror before she realized it wasn't Jackson.

Astrophel glanced up. He continued about his work, ignoring her. Ava moved to her knees, holding the jacket around herself, and inched forward. The dead body was shriveled, preserved like a mummy. Its mouth was wide open, head torn clean from its body and stitched back on. A set of fangs flashed in its mouth and she shivered.

Astrophel's son.

"So, let me guess," Ava snarled, more to keep her fear at bay than anything else. "I'm going to be your son's first meal?"

"He will be far too delicate to risk drinking such foul blood as from a shifter." Astrophel looked over at her again. He unfolded his long limbs and stretched his back. "You will serve a more glorious purpose."

"And what purpose is that?"

"Long ago, before your pathetic excuse of a civilization arose, everything belonged to vampires. We are the ageless gods, blessed to rule with strength and might." Astrophel let out a groan that sounded almost orgasmic, as though he was getting aroused by his own damned poetry. "Our people were glorious, rulers of the night. Blood flowed freely, and it was all ours for the taking. The master sat on his throne, and in his hands, he held the world."

Ava felt an unpleasant tingling in the back of her mind. The *master*? Astrophel was a king... who would he take orders from?

"Then the shifters came." A snarl ripped from the vampire. "The three she-devils of the day killed our master and destroyed all he had built. Three sacrifices must be made to return him. You are the first... the black panther. The lioness shall be next, and finally the kite. Then our master will rise again and devour the sun."

Astrophel opened his eyes and cocked his head to one side, smiling once more. "And my son will be by my side to witness the war that will end all shifters."

It was then that Ava felt real fear, coiled in the pit of her stomach. Whether or not she believed Astrophel was irrelevant. The fact of the matter was he believed it. He was going to kill them. And Jackson... Jackson would come for her, ensuring her death.

Don't, she wanted to scream at him, but even if he could hear her, he wouldn't listen. Not him with his thick-headed skull.

"He's... he's not going to come! I don't mean that much to him."

"When you carry his child, you don't mean much?"

She swallowed hard, her hands pressed to her stomach now. "I... I won't let you kill him!"

Astrophel laughed.

She knew it was laughable. Her eyes burned as she sank hopelessly back to the floor. "Why? Why a war, why... why can't you just accept what you've been given?"

"Because it was never yours to 'give'." Astrophel hissed between his teeth. "Shifters have decided that they are the dominant species, even though you are little but animals. You need to be taught a lesson—this is my planet. This place belongs to the vampires. Cities are nothing but our feeding grounds. Humans our slaves. And shifters? Shifters are our entertainment, to kill as we will."

"We are not animals."

"That's exactly what you are. Incapable of control. Breeding with any mutt that looks your way. You didn't even know Jackson's *name* before you let him fuck you."

Ava snarled again. Her panther stayed with her, bolstering her courage. "Jealous that nobody lets you fuck them?"

Astrophel growled once, low in his throat. He glanced toward the entrance of the cave, at the growing sunlight.

"I am a king," he said, under his breath. "And once the master rises, there will be none to oppose us."

Ava opened her mouth, but before she could speak, Astrophel's hand lashed out. He grasped her wrist and dragged her forward. His fangs sunk into her wrist and she screamed. He drank hungrily, making growling noises. Agony rolled up her arms, until she sagged against the bars. Her vision washed in and out.

The vampire sat back, licking his lips. He grinned as he stood and looked down at her.

"See you soon, Ava."

He turned and walked down the cave, disappearing into the darkness. Ava whimpered as she slumped to the ground. Sweat beaded on her brow despite the coolness of the cave. Her head spun, and her stomach revolted. There was nothing in it to vomit, though. When she glanced down, she saw the veins on her chest were a dark blue, spreading out down her torso and her arms. Had the vampire gone too far? Was this the feeling of her life seeping out of her? Killing her and her baby both...

Would he cry for me?

Jackson captivated her last thought as she fell into blackness, a picture of his face lulling her to sleep one last time.

Chapter Eight
Jackson

Jackson tossed the final vampire's body onto the roaring fire, then nodded, before he turned to Thunder and Val. The other alpha gave him a smirk and nodded once at him. Jackson ignored the motion, instead focusing on Val. She bandaged an open wound on her arm, not giving any indication she was in pain.

"Astrophel broke the treaty," Thunder said before Jackson could speak. "Typhoon is going to be out here in no time to deal with the corpse."

"And by then it will be too late for Ava." Jackson's heart pounded, and bile churned in his stomach. He couldn't leave her out there in that vampire's claws, waiting to be killed. "I'm going after them."

Thunder narrowed his eyes. "For real? This one girl is worth that? Acting against Astrophel with Typhoon's permission is one thing, but if you act without informing him—"

"If I inform him, he might tell me not to go."

Val let out an annoyed grunt as Thunder snorted. The other alpha looked incredulous, then a toothy grin formed on his face. "Wow. Didn't know you were one for suicide, Tornado. Going after Astrophel by yourself and against Typhoon's wishes? It's your funeral, bud. Been nice knowing you."

Jackson ground his teeth but nodded tensely toward Thunder. If their places were reversed, he'd be saying the same thing. They were alphas of separate chapters, united under Typhoon but far from being friends. There was a reason why Typhoon had sent him for these negotiations—he was the last person who'd help out someone on something like this.

He was unable to stop himself from giving out a biting remark, though. "Best run off to tell Daddy what happened, then."

Thunder rolled his eyes. He made a waving gesture and walked away without another word.

Jackson watched him go. His limbs were exhausted from the fight, muscles aching. Various cuts bled varying amounts. He wasn't in any shape to go up against Astrophel, and he knew it. He also knew that he wasn't going to let it end like this. He couldn't just abandon Ava. The image of her frightened eyes floated into his mind and his wolf snarled and batted against his chest.

He didn't realize Val was beside him until she dumped some rubbing alcohol on his shoulder, causing him to howl. She gripped him by the back of the neck and forced him to sit, then crouched beside him as she tended to his wounds.

"Are you going now?"

"Yes. Or, once I figure out where he is."

Val's expression faltered. She sucked in a deep breath and shook her head. "I should have grabbed the girl and handed her over to the corpse at the start of this."

Jackson snarled.

"What? You're going to run off and get yourself killed for her. And where will that leave me, Jackson? Huh? She's not worth dying for."

The truth was, everything inside of him told him that Ava was indeed worth dying for, that he would sacrifice himself for her in a heartbeat. He didn't want to tell Val that, didn't want to admit it, not even to himself.

Val scrubbed a hand over her eyes and glanced away. "He'll have taken her to where Mom and Dad were killed."

The words left a hollow, aching feeling in Jackson's chest. Val was the strongest person he knew. Without her, he never would have gotten to this point in his life. For her to show even this much vulnerability...

He shoved those thoughts aside. If he was killed, which he didn't plan on, then she'd be able to handle it. She would be alright. If Ava died? He wasn't sure that he'd be able to handle the guilt. It was his fault she was in this fucking mess to begin with, he wasn't going to abandon her!

"Why do you think he's there?" he asked his sister gruffly.

"He said he was going to resurrect his son with your blood. You killed him in that cave. Astrophel clearly expects you to find where he is. So. The cave."

Jackson was silent for a moment. He vividly recalled the cave. Darker than it should be, with flickering lights and black smoke choking the air. His parents, tied together in the center of a painted pentagram. The thick smell of blood. Astrophel's son with a knife in his hands, drawing it across his parents' throats while he and Val were held back, screaming.

Astrophel had laughed then. He hadn't laughed when Jackson tore his son's head from his body.

"If I drive through the night, I'll get there while there is still daylight."

"I'm not sure it matters." Val's expression twisted into one of pain and fear. "Is there anything I can do to convince you to wait?"

"He has her." It was all he needed to say.

The smoke from the pile of vampire bodies started to splutter, showing that they were about to combust. The siblings moved a little further from the bonfire. Val's distress showed in the lines of her face, but she shook her head.

"You know I can't go with you."

"I know."

"I can't leave my girls, Jackson. They need me, they need their mother."

"I know." Jackson turned to her and gripped her shoulders. "Take them to the safehouse. I want to make sure that they're safe. Going after Astrophel is going to cause a shitstorm and I don't want them caught up in it."

Val hesitated a moment before she nodded. She reached forward and touched his hand, a rare soft moment from his sister. She was usually hard as nails, showing little affection, though he knew that she always was and always would be protective of him, even though she was younger.

"Are you going to take the boys at least?"

Jackson shook his head. "It'll take too long. I can deal with him alone."

***

He arrived at the base of the cliff where the cave was located just as afternoon started to fade into evening. He had a couple hours of sunlight left, at most.

Jackson parked the bike and shifted before he began the long hike up the rocky hill. It was a hard climb, and by the time he got to the top, Jackson was sweating with effort. The cave loomed there, the same as before, with the scent of death billowing from it.

"Here goes nothing."

He crept into the cave mouth, squinting in the dark. His eyes roved for displaced shadows and his nostrils flared. The scent of blood and death was too strong for him to catch the sweet scent of vampire, though. He soon picked out a cage near the back, a huddled form inside.

Moving cautiously, Jackson made his way to it. Ava lay shivering inside, a jacket covering her naked body. Sweat stood out on her skin, which was a sickly green-yellow color. Jackson's heart leapt to his throat as he reached between the bars.

"Ava," he hissed, something hot sinking in his chest. "Ava, angel, wake up."

There was no response from her, no indication that she was alive but for her violent shudders. Jackson jerked on the bars of the cage, but they held solid. The door was padlocked, but if he was able to work the hinges free then maybe—

"Oops," came a voice behind him. Jackson swiveled around to see Astrophel standing there, a satisfied smirk on his face. "Looks like I went a bit overboard when I drank from her. I'm sorry that you weren't here to see it happen."

"Astrophel," Jackson snarled, springing to his feet.

Torches flared to life all around the edge of the cave, letting out a thick smoke that darkened it further. The sunlight at the mouth was almost completely obscured. Just behind the vampire was the mangled body of his son—Jackson would remember that face, even mummified as it was.

"So, what's the plan? You've broken the treaty with the Savage Brotherhood. They will come for you. Your kingdom can't withstand us."

Astrophel smirked. "You have grown weak, hiding the existence of vampires from even your own kind. We have only grown stronger. Do you think we kill every human that passes into our territory? No... better to cultivate them, to give us a continual supply of blood and new soldiers. And once you are dead, the Master will rise and then... oh, and then—"

Jackson sprang forward. Astrophel, caught off guard, was slow to dodge. Jackson was able to wrap a hand around the vampire's throat. Astrophel threw him back. Jackson snarled as he hit the cage. He shifted and sprang at the vampire again. Astrophel brought a fist down into Jackson's face, knocking him back once more.

Stop being reckless. He could almost hear Val's voice in his head.

Jackson crouched, watching Astrophel. The vampire grinned, laughed, and charged forward. This time, Jackson was ready. When Astrophel reached for him, he grabbed the vampire's wrist in his teeth and hurled him back. Astrophel rolled over his back, skittering to a stop just inside the mouth of the cave.

As Astrophel hissed and scrambled to his feet, Jackson threw himself at the vampire. They tumbled out of the cave into the last rays of sunlight. Astrophel let out a pained scream as bubbles burst along his skin. Jackson panted a moment before he closed his mouth around Astrophel's head. With a quick jerk, the vampire's neck snapped.

Astrophel's body twitched, unable to move. Jackson backed up, watching as his pale skin blackened and began to slough off. There was no more painful death for a vampire than this. But Astrophel deserved it. Deserved every second of it and worse.

Jackson shifted back to human form and loomed over the burning corpse. "Does it hurt, Astrophel?"

Does it hurt, little wolf? He had breathed at Jackson when his parents' blood mingled and stained the floor. *To see someone you love die and not be able to do anything about it?*

"Does it hurt?" Jackson repeated, his voice lower this time.

Astrophel's eyes roved before his body collapsed into a pile of ash. Jackson turned his back on the monster, the heaviness in his chest not abating at all. Not when Ava was still laying on the floor, unresponsive.

"Ava," he said again, louder this time, his voice desperate.

He searched around for the key to the cell door, finally finding it above the corpse of Astrophel's son. Jackson ignored it. He was already dead; there was no danger coming from that mummified body. Instead, he took the keys and rushed to Ava's cell. He unlocked it and pulled her into his arms.

Her heartbeat was faint but steady. There was a wound on her arm, with the green venom crusting the edge of two holes, but it looked clean. The lack of blood around it showed that Astrophel had drunk from her; he'd have sucked out the worst of the venom with it, then. Jackson pulled Ava into his arms, discarding the stinking jacket, and buried his face in her hair.

"It's going to be okay, Kitten," he promised. "I will make sure you're okay."

***

"Is she alive?"

Jackson grunted at Les as he carried Ava's unconscious form into the back of the bar. It wasn't as heavily charmed against vampire attacks as the safehouse, but he didn't want to expose his nieces to this. Les followed after him, the first aid kit in his hands. It had taken far too long to get here for Jackson's nerves. Now, as he laid Ava down and covered her naked body with a blanket, he saw she had stopped shivering.

"She's alive," he grunted as he checked her pulse. She had to be.

Relief washed over him as he felt the steady beat against his fingers.

There was a thudding noise behind him and both he and Les turned in time to see Cunningham storm into the backroom. His eyes blazed as he turned his gaze from Les to Jackson and, finally, to Ava. Rather than looking surprised, there came a tight, angry look on his face and he balled his fists.

"What the hell, Masters?"

Jackson reached for one of the spare pair of pants they had in the backroom and put them on before facing Cunningham. He wasn't going to do this naked. His muscles trembled as he gestured towards Ava.

"She was attacked by vampires."

Cunningham's jaw tightened. "She was bitten?"

Jackson didn't answer that.

Cunningham swore and grabbed the gun at his side. Jackson snarled, his whole frame growing larger to shield Ava from Cunningham's view. Without taking his eyes off the sheriff, he gestured at Les to leave. The bartender did so, looking more than grateful to get out of there.

"I don't want to do this, Jackson. But if she's been bitten, she's gonna turn into one of them."

"She's a shifter."

Cunningham pulled the gun from its holster. "Then she's going to go rabid."

"Astrophel bit her before and she pulled through. She's strong. I won't let you hurt her."

Cunningham growled under his breath. He studied Jackson for a long moment, the gun still in his hand. "I won't hesitate to put you down, too. Step aside and only one person has to die."

"You hurt her, and I will kill you. I've already killed Astrophel for her, do you think you'll be a challenge? We've all been bitten at one time or another, what right do you have to shoot her when you don't know what the venom will do to her?"

The sheriff holstered the weapon again. He let out a sigh, his shoulders sagging. Suddenly he looked... ancient. He ran a hand through his hair and moved closer. Jackson snarled in warning, but the sheriff ignored him.

"Astrophel is dead?"

"Yeah. Nothing but ash in the sunlight."

Cunningham nodded. "How is this going to affect things? Are we looking at war?'"

Jackson hesitated a moment. "Astrophel violated the treaty first. He hired the shifter who killed the vamp, then killed the shifter. Killing him means that his kingdom is up for grabs... I guess we'll know one way or another within a couple months. How'd you even know to come here?"

"Got calls about a naked man riding around with a naked, unconscious woman. Who else would it be but you?" Cunningham glanced at Ava again. "She can't stay here. If she goes rabid, I don't want her anywhere near civilians... I'll let you take charge of her, but if anybody gets hurt, it's on your head."

Jackson chewed his tongue to stop himself from snarling at him but nodded. "I'll take her to the safe house as soon as I can."

The sheriff watched him for a moment, then nodded. Without another word, he turned and left the backroom. Jackson let out a sigh of relief before turning his attention back to Ava. Retrieving a damp cloth, he began to wash the grime and blood from her body. It was very cold in the backroom, but when he went to turn up the temperature, Les stopped him.

"You overheat her and she'll shut down. You need to keep her cool."

After Les was gone, Jackson put another blanket over her—it just felt so wrong to see her shivering so violently. Then he slumped to the bed beside her. The greenish color was fading from her skin and her breathing was a bit smoother. Thank God for small blessings.

He leaned down to kiss her forehead, then her lips.

"I love you," he breathed, touching her cheek, kissing her softly again. "I love you, Ava."

She didn't answer, didn't move. Jackson held her hand, occasionally cooling her, staying up for hours on end holding her hand. He felt her pulse what seemed like every hour to make sure that her heart was still beating. Jackson felt completely broken, thinking about the idea that she might not wake up.

He couldn't imagine a world without her stubbornness and her beauty filling it with life. His wolf agreed, staying at the forefront of his chest. He continued his fitful vigil, eyes never moving from her face. At one point she began to stir, but her eyes stayed stubbornly shut and she fell back down to sleep.

Jackson kissed her again and waited for her to wake up.

Chapter Nine
Ava

Ava's fever was shorter than the previous one. Perhaps it was due to the fact that she was able to sleep through all of it, waking only to drink and eat before falling back under. She dreamt of Jackson holding a baby in his arms, a grin on his face. The warmth that filled her at that image was different from the burning of the fever.

When she finally woke feeling back to herself, it was almost heartbreaking to find him sitting beside her with no baby in sight. The dream quickly faded, though, as she realized how parched and weak she felt.

Jackson's face broke into a smile as she started to sit up. He helped her, hands lingering on her shoulders. "Hey. How are you feeling?"

"Alive... Are we at the safe house?"

"For now."

She shivered as she remembered Astrophel drinking from her. She checked her wrist, but all she saw were two red marks where he had bitten her. Jackson wrapped his arms around her and her panther purred.

"Oh!" Ava cried in relief as she put a hand to her chest. "She's still here."

Jackson pulled back slightly. "Your panther?"

"Yeah."

"I guess she feels safe, then." He nuzzled her neck. "Astrophel is dead."

Relief washed over her, but she didn't respond. Astrophel dead... what did that mean from here on out? Were the vampires going to descend on them now? Did it mean that they'd be cowed and hidden away? Did it mean that if Jackson left the Savage Brotherhood, Coalfell would still be safe?

Her heart sunk at the last thought. Of course, it wasn't going to be that easy. She threw back the blankets and made to stand. Jackson wasn't going to leave his life's work because she asked him to. And these last few days... how could she live like this, wondering if he was going to come home to her or be killed in battle?

And that wasn't even taking into account all the criminal activity he was involved in!

"I guess I can get out of here now," she said.

"What?" Jackson's surprised question made her flinch.

Ava didn't look at him. "The vampires won't be after me anymore. I can get back to my life."

"Oh... well, I suppose..."

She could see the reluctance in his eyes, the hesitance to let her go. It made her tense. She didn't need him to hold onto her. She had been just fine without him, and she'd be fine continuing on without him. All he had done was cause her trouble, really... Besides, it wasn't as though a few weeks in heart-stopping danger was enough to turn lust into love.

She turned away from him, blinking hard as she managed to stand.

It turned out to be a bit too much and she sank back down. With a shuddering breath, she wondered what she should say—she needed to start talking before he said something that neither of them could unhear.

"Is Shadow okay? And that other wolf?"

"They're both fine. I am, too, by the way. It's not like I took on a vampire king who was intent on killing me to resurrect his son..."

His teasing tone made her frown, but she didn't respond to it. A look of frustration crossed his face, and he glanced away. What was he hoping for? That she'd throw herself at his feet and beg him to keep her? Or was he just wanting to make her smile?

"I'm glad that you're okay," she finally said. "Astrophel said something to me... something about resurrecting the master who would unite all of vampire-kind and take over the world..."

"He's dead." Jackson reached for her hand and she pulled away from him. "You don't have to worry about anything he said, he's gone... Ava... these past few weeks—"

"I know," she said. "I know. It's been hard. I'm sorry—I didn't mean to be rude to you. I was just afraid."

He sighed. "Ava—"

"But now that it's over, we can go our separate ways, right? I can go back to my life and you can go back to your gang. No harm, no foul. I'll pretend like I've never heard of vampires and you can treat me like any other girl you've fucked. We don't even have to make eye contact in the grocery store."

Jackson's eyes widened. Then they narrowed, and his lips pulled into a tight line. "Why are you doing this, Ava?"

"Doing what?"

"Pushing me away."

Ava's hand started to move to her stomach, but she stopped herself. Was this the sort of life she wanted for her child? To grow up in a gang? Fighting vampires? No. And it wasn't what she wanted for herself, either. The tender look of desire and frustration in Jackson's face wasn't going to change that.

"I'm not pushing you away," she said finally. "I'm walking away. Because no matter what you have convinced yourself of, there is no future here. I told you I wasn't going to be a gangster's side piece."

"I'm not asking you to—"

"It's either that or you leave the Savage Brotherhood. Step down as alpha and let somebody else take the reins. And that would open us up to attack from vampires. Don't even pretend like you'd risk that for me. No... you have your job. I have my life. Now take me home."

Jackson looked like he might argue, but he didn't. Instead, he silently helped her down the stairs and onto his bike. A few minutes later they were on their way, things uncomfortably tense with her body pressed against his. Ava had a lump in her throat as she rode, trying to clear her mind, to think about anything but him. He pulled up to her place an hour later and she hopped off the bike, looking at him over her shoulder.

"Thank you," she said. She could see the pain in his eyes but bolstered herself. "Thank you for saving me. For protecting me."

"I will always be here to protect you," Jackson vowed.

Ava couldn't respond to that. She walked away, her heart feeling like it was going to explode with the loneliness and regret already welling up inside of her.

***

Melanie sat by her side, humming softly under her breath. Ava tapped her fingers on her thighs as she glanced around the waiting room. She and

Melanie were the only ones there, and for that she was grateful. Part of her felt silly for asking her friend to come with her, but she was too nervous to do it on her on.

She had been dreading this appointment for two weeks, ever since she had gotten home from the safe house and seen Jackson for the last time. After being poisoned by vampire venom twice, Ava wasn't sure what was going to happen with the baby. She had talked to Shadow about it once, who told her that she had been bitten three times while carrying her oldest daughter, but that didn't really soothe Ava's fears.

She was afraid that something had gone wrong, and that she would lose the only part of Jackson she had left.

"Ava?" came the voice of a nurse. Ava stood up, taking a deep breath as she followed the woman through the doorway and into an examination room. Melanie went with her, carrying her purse.

The doctor already waited for her and greeted her warmly. After making sure all the information he had was up-to-date, the doctor turned to her with a smile.

"So, you said on the phone that you were worried about being pregnant?"

"I am pregnant." The multiple home-tests she took proved that. "But, I—I got sick recently. I'm afraid that it—it put stress on the baby, maybe. I was very, very sick. I was practically in a coma. We're not sure what caused it. I was visiting my parents and... I got sick."

Beside her, Melanie shifted and frowned deeply. She didn't believe a word of it, but how was Ava meant to tell her the truth?

The doctor nodded. "Well, we will get an ultrasound technician in here shortly and take a look at things. How far along are you?"

"Uh... Two months. Maybe three?" Time was such a blur that she couldn't even remember what day it had been when she and Jackson had run together in the woods. It seemed like a lifetime ago.

The doctor nodded.

Within a little while, Ava was laying on the examination bed, her shirt rolled up over her belly. Cold gel spread over her stomach as the doctor pressed the wand against it. Ava held her breath as she watched the screen, her eyes darting toward the doctor's face.

"See that?" she said, pointing at a spot on the screen. "That's her heart."

A burst of relief washed over her. Melanie gripped her shoulder, smiling.

Ava stared at the tiny pulsing thing. "Is she okay?"

"Looks okay to me," the doctor said. "We can do some blood work, but that's a healthy pulse if I've ever seen one."

Her muscles relaxed and she leaned back. Her baby was okay. It seemed like a miracle, but there it was. They were going to be fine. The question was what was she going to do now—staying in Coalfell didn't seem like a good idea. Not when Jackson was right there. If he saw her pregnant and put it together... she wasn't sure she was strong enough to walk away a second time.

Melanie drove her home silently. When they passed by the bar, Ava couldn't stop herself from looking over at it. Jackson's bike was nowhere to be seen, and she slumped back again.

"Are you coming to work tomorrow?" Melanie's voice was a fake upbeat.

"Yeah. Why wouldn't I?"

"Well, you did disappear for two months and then came back pregnant. You're lucky you were given your job back."

Ava flinched at the accusation in her voice. She did consider herself lucky to have been given her job back, indeed. Jackson had faked an official-looking document detailing her time in a hospital, and her boss had been very worried. He assured her that she was welcome to return. And she needed the money, what with a baby on the way...

Once they were back in her house, Melanie made them both some tea while Ava slumped into the couch. She was so exhausted lately that she wasn't certain if she had recovered from the venom. Maybe it was just normal pregnancy stuff.

Melanie brought her the tea. Catnip. Ava took a deep whiff of it. It calmed her instantly, her panther stretching and purring at the familiar scent. Melanie lapped at hers, looking very cat-like as she did so. Her legs curled under her and her eyes remained locked on Ava.

Eventually, Ava sighed and set her tea down. "What do you want to know?"

"Where you really were."

Ava looked away. "I was sick."

Melanie narrowed her eyes.

"I *was* sick." A lump rose in her throat. "But... but there is more than that. I wasn't with my parents. I was with... a man. And he..."

Tears started to roll down her face. Melanie's accusing expression turned to one of horror and sympathy. She moved forward, taking Ava's hands in hers.

"You can tell me. Is he... the baby's father?"

"Yes."

"Who—"

"It doesn't matter," Ava said, cutting her off. She didn't want to talk about Jackson, didn't even want to mention his name. She had pushed him away completely so that he was lost to her, and now she would be raising their child by herself. "I can't have him. Oh, my God! I want him. I want him so bad."

The tears increased. Shock, then relief, flitted over Melanie's face.

"So you were with him willingly?"

Ava opened her mouth then closed it. Not exactly willingly, but not the way that Melanie had been fearing, either. She let out a shuddering breath as she fought to regain control of herself.

Since she had lost him, Ava thought about Jackson constantly. All she wanted was to see him, yet every time she drove past the bar and saw his motorcycle, she kept driving rather than stopping to see him. Ava wondered if he even thought about her at all—then she wondered why it should even matter to her. She made her choice. She had to leave it at that. A life of gangs and violence... it wasn't for her.

"Hey." Melanie wrapped her arms around Ava. "It's going to be okay. I'm going to be here for you, understood? I'm here for you. You're not alone."

Ava nodded, forcing a tremulous smile on her face. Her parents had said the same thing when she told them about her pregnancy. But the thing was, she wasn't alone because she had been abandoned. She had been the one doing the abandoning.

The thought broke down the rest of her defenses and she collapsed into Melanie's arms.

"I love him," she sobbed. "I love him but I can't have him."

Melanie held her while she cried for what seemed like hours. Eventually, the sobs turned to sniffles, and she was able to pull away from her friend. The truth of everything that happened pressed against the back of her teeth, but she knew she couldn't tell Melanie what had happened without going into the vampires. It was so unbelievable she knew that Melanie would never accept it.

"Do you want to talk about it?"

Ava ran a hand through her hair. It was greasy. When was the last time she had showered? Two days? Ugh. There was no need for her to start falling apart over this. No, she was tougher than that. Starting tomorrow, she was going to get her life back to normal... even though she knew there was no normal left.

She thought about Jackson, his mouth, the way he touched her, fighting the thoughts out of her head. She knew she had to get rid of him for good, that it would do no good to dwell, but Ava found it was almost impossible to move on.

"We met at the bar," she said slowly. "And it was... it was like a movie. Just everything about him clicked with everything about me. I ran away with him, I thought that I'd found..." What had she thought she'd found? "And then

I found out he was part of the gang. And I can't live like that, so I left him."

Melanie's eyes widened. "Did he hurt you?"

"No. He let me go." She turned her gaze to the two cups of tea, now cold. "He let me go."

***

The months flew by. Ava pushed Jackson from her mind and focused on taking care of herself. Her belly grew bigger and rounder week by week, and pretty soon she had people at the coffee shop asking her when she was due and being offered a place to sit regularly. Her dedication to her job didn't go unnoticed, and it was soon bearable work. As the time drew closer for her to give birth, she was pleased to see that she had racked up the savings she needed in order to take time off when the baby was born.

One night after a long day, she went home and curled up on the couch, her hands pressed against her stomach as the baby kicked. She had just started to doze off when the door was flung open. Jackson came charging in.

Her heart jumped into her throat as she got to her feet. "Jack—"

His gaze focused on her belly, then darted back to her face. "You have to come with me. Now."

Chapter Ten
Jackson

Jackson sat at the bar, taking a shot of the cheap whiskey he'd ordered, something to wash the taste of her out of his mouth. He closed his eyes, and again, despite himself, her face flitted behind his lids, a soft smile or a scowl, those beautiful, angry eyes. He sighed as he opened his eyes again, putting a cigarette between his lips and lighting it. He took a long drag as Les came over to him.

"Another shot?" he asked.

Jackson shook his head, gesturing to his bottle of beer instead. He wasn't trying to give himself a headache, even though it was how he seemed to end each day no matter how much he drank.

He'd lost everything. After he killed Astrophel, he had thought everything was going to be okay. That finally he'd feel at peace, that for the first time in his life he was going to have a future to look forward to. Then Ava had left. He had been so certain she'd stay, but she left...

And then there were the vampires. His actions had stirred up the vampires to a frenzy; things had calmed down now, but several of the other kings had been talking about declaring an all-out war. Astrophel's kingdom had been consumed by the others. Still, it had been hard work keeping them out of shifter territory. Without leadership, they ran rampant. His crew had had to kill vampires left and right as they snuck into the town. The other chapters were facing the same issues.

Once the vampires got their own under control, Typhoon had arrived. The alpha of the Brotherhood had been furious. He stripped Jackson of his title and Jackson was frankly surprised that Typhoon didn't kill him. He was disgraced, allowed to come to the bar only because Les was such a good friend of his parents.

Even so, whenever he walked through the doors, the others, members of the gang that used to look up to him with pride and trust in their eyes, always turned away. Shuffling back outside, heads hanging. He couldn't blame them, not really, but it still hurt.

Les brought Jackson the beer and set it down in front of him. He looked like he was going to say something, but only shook his head and turned away. Jackson cracked open the beer and began to gulp it down when his phone started buzzing.

Annoyed, he pulled it out. Val. Again. She was calling him more often these days. Typhoon had made her the alpha in his place. While Jackson was glad that it went to someone who had the strength and smarts to actually be an alpha, it didn't stop his wolf from snarling every time she called him to watch the girls. It was because she was off pulling missions or fighting vampires. While he was no longer invited to the party.

He thought about declining but answered anyway. He adored his nieces, and quite frankly didn't trust anybody else with them these days. Not when some members of the gang might be looking to topple Val and claim the spot of alpha themselves.

"Shadow," he grunted in greeting.

"Bring Ava to the safehouse."

Jackson sat up a little straighter. A tingle ran down his spine and his hands clenched. "Why?"

"Don't be an idiot, Jackson. Did you really think that the vampires would let her go just because Astrophel was dead? The kings want her. They say that because you killed Astrophel, they need her to resurrect his son to be king. But we both know that's bullshit."

A tremor ran down his spine as he remembered what Ava had told him. They needed to sacrifice a panther, a lioness, and a kite. Were they still determined that Ava would be their panther?

"Typhoon's agreed to this?"

"The vamps are threatening to come at us full-force. He says even if we are able to defeat them, the loss of life will be catastrophic. He's headed your way. Get her to the safe house now. I'll meet you there."

He didn't question why Val was suddenly for protecting Ava. Instead, he hung up his phone and dashed out of the bar, shouting over his shoulder for Les to put it on his tab. He leapt onto his bike and raced towards Ava's house.

Her scent enveloped him as he rushed inside. Ava squealed and jumped to her feet. Her face paled as one hand reached out toward him.

"Jack—"

She cut off. Her blouse clung to her figure, showing off her rounded pregnant belly. Something inside of him twisted, but he didn't waste time on emotion. Not now. Instead, he moved toward her.

"You have to come with me. Now."

She didn't speak. She stood there with a surprised look on her face, her hands on her smooth, rounded stomach.

"Ava..."

"Hi," she said softly.

He couldn't do anything but stand there and stare at her, drinking her in, the sight of her face like a dream to him. Then he went to her, taking her face in his hands, pulling her in for a soft, hot kiss, one that he needed. He kissed her again, then again before she started to respond, breathing against his lips, her eyes closed as she tasted his mouth in return. Jackson breathed her in, wrapping his arms around her, feeling the hard, roundness of her belly against his abdomen. He continued to kiss her, his head spinning as he smiled against her lips.

The vampires were coming. He pulled back and shook his head. "There isn't time for this. We have to go."

"What?" Ava blinked in confusion. "Why?"

"I'll explain. I guess we have to take your car, you're too huge for my bike."

Ava's jaw dropped. "Excuse me?" she spluttered.

"Ava, please. Please just trust me."

He held his breath as he stared up at her. For a moment, he thought she was going to refuse. But then she nodded; he let out a sigh of relief. Without another word, he took her wrist, a pleasant thrill going through him at the touch of her skin, and pulled her from her home.

She cradled her stomach as they drove. His gaze flickered towards it. She sat tense, staring straight ahead. Eventually, Jackson cleared his throat.

"How have you been?" he asked.

"Pregnant."

"I see that... mine?"

She nodded stiffly. He sighed. Of course, it wasn't going to be as easy as just starting back up where they had left off. His grip on the steering wheel was so tight his knuckles were white. Releasing a shaky breath, he tried to relax.

"Were you going to tell me?"

She glanced over at him. "No."

"Why?"

"You know why."

Jackson hesitated for a moment. The truth of what had been happening pressed against his lips, but he didn't want her to feel like he was blaming her for what had happened. Instead, he let out a shaky sigh and nodded.

"I know why."

Ava's shoulders sagged slightly. She glanced at him from the corner of her eye and swallowed hard. "It's a girl."

A girl. A smile spread across his face. "What are you going to name her?"

"I haven't decided," Ava said. "Any ideas?"

Something like hope flickered through Jackson. He swallowed, mind flitting over the possibilities. "Uh... Snow?"

Ava laughed softly. "Like Snow White?"

He shrugged. "What about Ella, then?"

"I never knew you were into fairy tales." Ava's laugh deepened, but it cut off abruptly. When he glanced at her, concerned, he saw deep fear in her expression. "Jackson... are the vampires really coming after me again?"

"Yes. I won't let them touch you, I swear. They will not touch you."

Ava nodded and fell silent again. The quiet between them was tense, full of energy. Jackson found himself wanting to tell her everything, wanting to beg her to take him back. But he knew it wasn't fair. He couldn't make it seem like she had an obligation to be with him.

"So... are you okay?"

Something snapped inside of him. His voice cracked as he answered. "No, Ava. I have not been okay. I've been the fucking opposite of okay."

Ava narrowed her eyes at him. "There's no need to take that tone."

Jackson focused on the road, breathing deeply. "Sorry. It's just... a lot happening. Ava, I..." He *couldn't* tell her about being kicked from the gang... "Ava, if I wasn't part of the Savage Brotherhood... would you have told me?"

She tensed and glanced away. "I...
I don't know. Maybe. But you can't. It's
too important to you."

"Don't you think that should be my
decision?"

Ava turned her face toward the
window beside her and said nothing.

He let out a deep sigh, relaxing his
grip on the wheel again. "So... So I met
this woman. At the bar."

She tensed, shoulders hunching
forward.

Jackson reached over to take her
hand, lacing his fingers with hers. "She
was beautiful. Perfect. And she was
wild—she ran with me. She let me touch
her. She let me see who she was. I'd
never known anybody like her. It
seemed like we were always locking

horns. She never let me get away with anything, and I loved it."

Ava didn't say anything, but she turned back to him. She dragged her teeth over her bottom lip.

"I lost that woman," Jackson said. "The moment I got her. I never got to see her run again and I barely got to see her smile. I lost her. That is what's wrong, Ava. I know that I wasn't good enough for her, didn't deserve her. But, God, do I love her."

Ava gasped softly. "Jackson..."

"Don't say anything. Not right now. Please. Just let me hold your hand and pretend everything is going to be okay."

"Jackson—" she began again, but she cut herself off as they turned down the long road in the forest that led to the safe house.

They pulled up to the house to see that nobody was there yet. Jackson frowned. He'd expected to see Val, at least. Still, an empty house meant that he had time to fully explain to Ava what was happening. He helped her inside, his arm around her waist as he looked around them. Every shadow seemed like a threat and his wolf snarled, wanting to tear through anything that threatened their mate.

Once they were in the house, Ava broke away from him. She waddled—honest to God waddled—to the couch and sat down. Her hands rubbed her belly as she stretched her legs out. A faint blush washed over her cheeks as she glanced at him through her lashes.

"What can I get for you?" Jackson asked. "Anything?"

"Um, some water would be good," she said shyly.

Jackson hurried to get it, bringing it back to her, watching as she took a long sip. His attention seemed to unnerve her, so he looked away. Finally, he knew that he couldn't delay it any longer.

"Ava... there are some things you should know. It's not just the vampires who are coming after you."

Editing out the fact that he wasn't the alpha anymore, he told her everything. As he spoke, her eyes widened and her cheeks drained of color. By the time he was done, her arms were firm around her stomach and she shivered violently.

"Should we be here, then?" her voice was little more than a whisper. "If the gang turns on you—"

"Don't worry about it." Her words made him frown, though. That was a valid concern. He wasn't the alpha any longer. Val would have his back, he was certain of it, but the others? When it was them against Typhoon... what would they do? "Try to get some rest, Ava. I won't let anything happen. I promise."

He moved to the front porch to keep an eye out. Once he closed the door, he took a deep breath. If he couldn't count on the gang to back him up, then there was only one person who would possibly help him. He hated having to dial that number, but Ava was worth everything.

"Coalfell police department, Sheriff Cunningham speaking," the sheriff said when he answered the phone. "How can I help you?"

If he knew who was calling him, Jackson didn't think he'd be so cordial. "Blizzard. It's Tornado."

A moment of silence followed. "Masters. What the hell is this?"

"I need your help." The words weren't as difficult as he thought they would be. "At the safe house. I... I've gotten myself into a mess and I need you."

Cunningham snorted. "Me? Really? You must be an idiot if you think that I'm going to help you, Masters. What happened? You bring the feds down on you? Or are you dealing with a coup? I heard chatter that Shadow was running the gang. She finally get sick of having to put up with you?"

"It's not like that at all. It's... I've been kicked out, sheriff. I went against Typhoon's orders and I killed Astrophel. Now the other vampire kings want retribution. But they're not after me," he quickly said as the sheriff grunted. "They're after a civilian. She's pregnant. I don't know how much time I've got. I won't let them hurt her, and Typhoon will kill me himself for this. So, if you can't fight... then at least come get her. Take her away from here, put her in witness protection. Something."

The sheriff was silent for a long time. "Vampires and Typhoon, huh? This isn't my battle, Masters. It's your job to take care of this. What the hell are you doing, to get yourself tangled in this mess?"

Jackson closed his eyes. "Please. Please, Cunningham. For her. Please."

For one moment, he was certain that his begging was going to be for nothing. But then the sheriff sighed. It was a defeated sound that made Jackson's heart leap. Maybe they had a shot at this after all.

"I'll be there," he grumbled and hung up the phone.

Jackson shoved his phone back into his pocket. His heart beat wildly, but there was a measure of relief, too. Val was going to give him shit for this but he already knew it was going to end in violence. Typhoon didn't like to be questioned. And if he had already decided to give Ava to the vampires? There would be no changing his mind.

He released a pent-up breath and nodded to himself. This was happening. But he was ready to meet it, head-on.

The roar of cycle engines broke through the dusk, and within a few moments, four bikes appeared. He tensed, searching them to see if they were friend or foe. The four of them stopped at the porch. Val got off her bike, followed by Basil, Eric, and Les.

Val stormed up the steps and glowered at him. "I hope she's worth it, Jackson."

He grinned at her. "You're the one who called me, remember?"

"Whatever." Val turned to the men. "Secure the perimeter and keep watch. I want to know before Typhoon gets here, got it? Tornado, inside. We need to talk."

Chapter Eleven
Ava

Ava looked up warily as Val entered. The other woman gave her a slight nod before turning to Jackson, who had come in after her. Jackson gave Ava a brief smile before he focused on his sister. The two of them eyed each other with enough tension to strangle a man. Ava tried to curl up as small as possible.

Eventually, Val spoke. "You look like shit, Jack. What have you been doing, sleeping in a gutter?"

Jackson scowled. "We're not here to discuss that, Val. Typhoon's coming, how do we stop him from giving Ava to the vamps?"

"Easy. You challenge him instead of backing down like a little shit and you take leadership of the Coalfell chapter back."

Ava's eyes widened and she couldn't stop herself from gasping. Both of them looked at her, Val with annoyance and Jackson with a flinch. She pressed both of her hands to her mouth. Jackson had been replaced as Alpha of the Coalfell chapter? Why hadn't he told her? Was that why he asked her if she'd have told them about their baby if he wasn't part of the gang?

"Maybe I don't want it back," Jackson said, his voice low. "Maybe I have something more important to fight for."

Val snorted once and turned to Ava. "You. Panther girl. Do you love him?"

"I—What?" Ava spluttered. "Why would you ask—"

"I'd say it was quite obvious. Do you love my brother?"

Ava tried not to look at Jackson. She really tried. But he drew her like a magnet, those hopeful eyes locking with hers. Her baby kicked inside of her and she pressed both hands to her stomach. It felt like the whole world hinged on her answer.

"...Yes," she whispered. "I love you, Jackson. But I stand by what I said before, I can't be a gangster's side piece—"

"Side piece?" Val snorted, but she smiled. "Try being his mate, then. If you're worried about the baby, don't be. My three girls know nothing about the gang. They just think they have a cool momma who rides on motorcycles. Trust me, if your kid is anything like my big brother, they'll find a way into the gang with or without an introduction."

Ava fell silent, still looking into Jackson's hopeful gaze. Eventually, she couldn't look at him anymore and turned her face away. It was impossible... wasn't it? There were just too many reasons why they couldn't get together...

"Before my love life sidetracks things too much..." Jackson shook his head. His voice was low and raspy. He cleared his throat. "Val, I've called in backup."

She tensed. "Backup?"

"Yeah."

Val loomed closer. Though Jackson was taller and far more muscular, she was a pretty intimidating sight. Ava was glad that she didn't have to be on the end of that look as she glared at her brother. Her fists clenched, metal studs standing from the knuckles of her black leather gloves.

Jackson's voice was perfectly even as he spoke. "Cunningham is on the way here."

Ava got to her feet, wondering if Val would strike out if she put herself between them. The baby kicked harder and she knew she couldn't risk it. The fury on Val's face was terrifying. If that was directed at her, Ava would have been running as fast as she could.

"The cop?" Val spat. "You're bringing a cop into this? This is gang business and—"

"This is far beyond gang business. This is about me protecting Ava... our child..." Jackson glanced at her. "I can't let anything happen to them. Even if it means bringing in the likes of Cunningham."

"The traitor."

"He's a shifter, Val. And a powerful one. We need his help."

"He's a prick," Val said, her face wrinkled up in disgust.

"Yeah, I know," Jackson said. "But he's what we've got."

Val hummed for a moment before she spat on the floor. "Fine. Whatever. But he doesn't change things. When

Typhoon arrives, you fight him. You beat the fuck out of him, and you reclaim your position of alpha of the Coalfell chapter. And then we can deal with the vamps the way we see best. They're not going to push the issue over one shifter. Typhoon just doesn't want to concede territory."

All this over her. Ava shuddered, even though she fought against it. She strode forward, pulling up her best bravado. "Then that fucker can go to hell!"

Her face flared bright red. Jackson laughed out loud, and even Val smirked. Ava glared at the both of them. "What? I swear when the situation calls for it. And as for the two of you, you better not use that language around this baby once it's born!"

Jackson turned to her, a smile breaking across his face. "That means you'll stay?"

The hope in his eyes made her melt. Her body burned for his, and she couldn't stop herself from flinging herself into his arms. Vampires, gangs, whatever else. There was nothing powerful enough to make her walk away again. Her eyes burned with determination as she nodded. Whatever happened, she would deal with it.

Jackson seized her around the waist. He spun her around, laughing, before he set her down again. His eyes glowed as his hands gently stroked her face. Then, moving slowly, he pressed a kiss to her mouth. She moaned and flung her arms around his neck.

"Yuck." Val's footsteps retreated.

The two ignored her, too focused on one another. Jackson suckled on her lower lip. Ava responded to him eagerly, molding her body to his as she had desperately wanted to for the past few months. All the lies she had told herself right after she left—that she could never be in a relationship with someone she was so up and down with, that it would only drive her crazy, that he was a criminal even if he was a hero, a dark man with a dark sense of himself—all fell away. She was his, fully and completely.

Her panther yowled in agreement and she could hear the distant echo of a howling wolf. They broke apart, smiling at one another. Jackson combed his fingers through her hair, so soft and gentle. When he lowered his hand again, it brushed against hers, and she found herself linking their fingers together. The skin contact was electric, something Ava felt throughout her entire body.

"We're going to do this," he promised her. "And those corpses will never, ever get their hands on you again. I promise."

"I know," she whispered.

And she fell into him again. His hands were all over her, hers all over him, ripping at their clothing. Soon every stitch was pooled on the floor, bodies naked and pressing together. Her swollen breasts, heavy and aching, needing to be touched, squished against his chest. Their mouths sought each other out, hungry. Ava panted and moaned as he laid her on the couch.

Gentle hands caressed her belly.

"We're going to have to do this another way, aren't we?" he asked. "Turn onto your side."

Ava obeyed without a word. Jackson kissed her shoulder, his hands still caressing her body. She ached so badly for him that she almost lost her breath. It had been too long since she had had him near her like this.

He nuzzled into her thigh as he lifted her leg up to prop it on the edge of the couch. "You're so beautiful. So perfect."

"Jackson—"

Ava was cut off when he started his work. She tried to keep her legs still, to keep her body from shaking and squeezing him. Ava's breath was lost as she gasped and squirmed against his face, trying to spread her legs, to buck

238

away from the intense pleasure. He wouldn't let her, but continued to send pleasure bursting through her body. She felt like she was on fire, her fingers digging into his hair.

"Jackson," she panted when he pulled his face away, mouth wet, eyes hungry as he pulled her up to kiss her stomach.

He sat on his heels, licking his lips. Ava got the chance to look at his perfect body once again. He was so chiseled, his body strong and powerful, the lines of his chest and his arms thick and sturdy. She stared at him with her eyes half-lidded, feeling like she had never wanted anything more than she wanted him.

"Now..." Jackson sat on the couch and pulled her into his lap.

"No," she said, kneeling. "No, I'm pregnant, I'm too—"

"Say you're too heavy and I'll spank you."

The image sent pleasant chills through her, and Ava was almost tempted to say it again just to get the promised spanking. She braced herself on the couch and shook her head.

Jackson's gaze softened. "I'm a big boy, Ava. And this will be more comfortable for you."

She gazed into his eyes and nodded. She lowered herself down slowly, taking him deep, holding her breath as she sank down on top of him. He was so thick and long, so perfect inside of her. She moved experimentally, rocking her hips back and forth.

"Come on, kitten," he purred. "Make yourself feel good."

He didn't have to ask Ava twice. She moved on top of him in a feverish rhythm, losing every bit of self-consciousness she'd had the moment she looked into his eyes and saw nothing but adoration and lust as he looked up at her naked body, occasionally taking one of her nipples between his lips, sucking on it while they moved together.

Eventually, the trembling and heat twisting inside of her was too much to bare and she had to stop. Jackson pulled her into his arms, kissed her deeply, and then moved them both so she was laying back on the couch, her ass half-off while he braced himself against her hip. He moved in and out slowly, shallowly, while he kissed her neck.

"My perfect girl," he moaned. "Are you mine now, Ava? All mine?"

"Yes," she breathed, tangling her fingers in his hair once more. "Are you mine?"

"Forever."

He kissed the back of her neck, sinking his teeth into it slightly as he moved faster. Ava moaned loudly, eager to take him, and ended up finishing just moments before he did. Ava felt like she was glowing as he slowed down, pulling out, holding her body back against his chest.

"Thank you for coming back," Jackson said in a soft voice. "Thank you for being mine."

She pressed herself against him, sweat on her brow, a smile on her face. "I love you, Jackson."

He kissed her tenderly. "I love you, too. So much."

***

It was sometime later that the sheriff came to the safe house. Jackson greeted him with relief, even if he was a bit stiff. Ava had seen him in the coffee shop from time to time but never would have thought that Cunningham would have been connected to the Savage Brotherhood. Now he had a handgun strapped to his thigh and carried a shotgun over his shoulder.

Val glared at Cunningham, who glared right back at her.

"Val," he said stiffly.

"Cunningham. How good to see you," Val said sarcastically. "It was nice of you to show up."

"I wouldn't have had to show up if your brother could handle his business."

Val snarled at him, moving forward. Jackson stepped between them and shot his sister a look that had her moving back. Her hands clenched and Ava couldn't help but wonder if all of this was a good idea. The tension was just getting thicker... as she sat on the couch, she wondered why she hadn't just told Jackson they needed to get on a plane and go to Costa Rica. Avoid all this.

"Thank you for coming, Gabriel," Jackson said.

"I didn't come for you. I came because you said there was a civilian in danger." Cunningham's eyes lit on her. "You her?"

Ava held out her hand. "I'm—"

"Ava, I know. I go to the coffee shop you work at regularly. So how did you get mixed up with this?"

"Astrophel decided he wanted to kill me."

Cunningham gave her a critical look. She knew, somehow, that he'd already worked out that she was pregnant with Jackson's child. She met his gaze and it softened a little as he nodded.

"I hope you understand what you're getting into," he told her. "Cause this isn't a life that stops at the doorway. You stay with this ugly mug," he jabbed his thumb at Jackson, "and you're in it for life. You'll always be fighting vampires, the law, and the gang itself from time to time. Every time you say goodbye could be your last time to see him."

Val snorted. "Tell us how you really feel."

"You know it's true."

Ava gazed steadily at the sheriff. "I love him. Love is enough."

Cunningham considered her for a moment, then nodded. He turned back to Jackson. "So, what are we facing? Typhoon alone or is he bringing vampires with him?"

"I arranged a meeting," Val snapped. "To discuss the situation. But we're not gonna get anywhere by talking. Jackson will—"

A booming voice spoke from behind him. "No talking? Then why am I here?"

Ava shivered at the voice. She turned to see a gigantic man standing in the doorway. He was flanked by two others who narrowed their eyes at the group. The doors behind them burst in and one of the guards Val brought with her rushed in.

"Boss, I—"

Val held up a hand. The man paled as he saw the people already in the room. She snarled at him, and he backed up a step.

The big man, Typhoon, took a step toward Ava. His gaze fell on her stomach and he let out a soft curse. "Pregnant. Tornado, you are one stupid—"

"I'm not going to let you take her." Jackson stepped in front of her. Breaking free of that gaze, she felt like she could breathe again. Her fingers pressed into Jackson's back. She could feel him trembling. "I may have backed down when you removed me as Alpha of the Coalfell Chapter, but this ends here. I'm not letting you take her."

Typhoon glanced at him, then Val, Cunningham and finally at Ava. "I can delay them long enough for her to have the kid."

"You will cede territory in exchange for her life." Jackson stood straighter. "Or I challenge you as the Alpha."

Typhoon stared at him for a long moment before he laughed. "This is a turn... I accept your challenge, Masters.

Now... you have five minutes to say your goodbyes and then I'm going to kill you."

Chapter Twelve
Jackson

Jackson forced himself to stay calm as they headed outside. Typhoon was bigger than him, stronger, more experienced. Basically head and shoulders above him. But that didn't matter.

I'm fighting for my mate, he thought, casting a glance back at Ava. He smiled at her. Her face was utterly white as she held her belly. He stopped and pressed a kiss to her forehead.

"I'll be fine."

"Jackson..."

"I'll be fine," he repeated.

Typhoon waited for him in the yard, a smirk on his lips. As Jackson started forward, though, the house shuddered. The ground shook and a renting noise like thunder filled the air. Light flashed in the sky. The shifters all froze, looking around with wide eyes.

"Vampires," Jackson muttered. "They must have broken the charm."

In the next moment, dark figures dropped from the sky. Jackson shoved Ava, sending her back inside. Then he shifted, shaking off his clothes as he did so. The vampires dropped over them, hisses filling the air.

Jackson moved quickly, launching himself at the closest vamp, latching onto its legs with his massive jaws. He sank his teeth in, ripping the flesh away so that the vampire fell to the ground with a scream. Jackson ripped his leg off with one final bite, then the other, moving on to the next vampire while the other one remained crippled on the ground.

Val snarled in her jaguar form, leaping over him to tackle a vampire. The others tackled vampires, but more kept coming. Typhoon shifted into a huge, menacing wolf and threw back his head, howling. It reverberated through the forest, making all the vampires shiver. Jackson's wolf rose in challenge to the sound, urging him to tackle the other alpha; it was an instinct he'd never had before.

He ignored it for now, quickly ripping the head off of one vampire before he tore into the throat of another. Out of the corner of his eye, Jackson saw Ava, her belly heavy, sink low to the ground in the doorway. She had shifted, her black fur gleaming. A vampire crouched before her.

Jackson lunged, but another vampire side-swiped him, preventing him from getting to help her. His wolf howled.

Ava sprang forward. Her claws gleamed in the night as she savaged the vampire; it screamed and jerked, and she dug her teeth deep into its throat, choking it out. Val joined her, tearing the head clear off. She stood protectively before Ava, taking out any vampires that came at them.

His distraction cost him. He felt fangs penetrate his neck but jerked away in time, flipping around, snarling at the vampire. Another wolf—Cunningham— slinked up behind the vampire, diving at him from the back so that he fell to the ground. Jackson shook himself. Venom seeped into his bloodstream but he ignored it for now. A good half-dozen vampires were focused on Typhoon. He moved this way and that, slashing and snapping at them. He was able to kill several before more flooded the area; they separated him from his men.

There were screams in the air, vampires and shifters, the snarl of a lion as Basil crushed a vampire in his jaws. Jackson got a moment to look for Ava, frantically scanning the space for her. His eyes landed on hers as she crouched behind Val.

Cunningham leapt onto the back of a vampire headed for Val. Jackson was torn for one moment before he leapt back into the fray, charging in to help Typhoon. Cunningham and Val would protect Ava; without Typhoon, the whole Brotherhood would crumble.

A vampire was on Typhoon's back. Jackson locked his jaws around its leg and yanked it back. It rolled several times before springing back to its feet. By that time Jackson was already fighting back-to-back with Typhoon, tearing and slashing at the vampires all around them. The venom worked its way into his head, making everything whirl around him. Something tore into his side and he collapsed, blackness whirling around him.

***

Ava's scent enveloped him. He moaned, reaching blindly for her. He found a hand and held it tightly, but it wasn't Ava's. It was too big. Too... heavy. Jackson managed to force his eyes open to find that it was Cunningham's hand that he gripped so tight. With a grunt, Jackson pushed it away.

"Ava."

"Easy." Cunningham sounded exhausted as he put a hand on Jackson's shoulder. "She's right here."

Then he saw her. Relief washed over him and he reached for her. She bent over him, her lips pressing against him again and again. He wanted to tell her to be gentle but was too drawn in by her affection to discourage it. Everything threatened to spin around him again, but he managed to sit up.

He sat on the couch in the safe house. Cunningham and Val were both there, as were Typhoon's men. When he saw Jackson was awake, he slipped from the room.

"How long have I been out?"

"Few hours," Cunningham grunted. There was a bandage around his arm. He stood and stretched, yawning. "Glad to know I don't have to kill you, boy. Seems like you've finally built up an immunity to vampire venom."

Jackson grunted. He fingered the holes in his neck, finding them not much more than shallow scratches. If they had been any worse, he probably wouldn't have made it. Not with venom in the neck. He pushed that thought aside as he turned to Ava. She appeared unharmed, but he looked over her carefully, making sure that she hadn't been hurt. When he was satisfied, he pulled her back with him and held her in the crook of his arm.

His eyelids fluttered open then, and he looked up at her face in wonder.

"Lily," he said. "I like the name Lily."

Ava choked on a sob of relief, kissing him again and again.

"Lily," she said softly. "I like it."

"Good," he said, then promptly fainted again.

***

He woke again sometime later, feeling much lighter. Ava's scent was still there. This time he kept his eyes closed, waiting for his strength to recover. There were footsteps nearby and then Ava spoke softly.

"Thank you."

"No problem," Cunningham said.

Ava hummed. "You were bitten, too. I saw you."

"Yeah. No big deal. It doesn't really get me like it does other shifters."

"Why not?"

Cunningham grunted. "Lucky, I guess."

Jackson thought about cracking open an eye, but stayed still. If he was honest, Cunningham's mysterious immunity had always been a curiosity to him. He never knew why. He was certain Cunningham did, but the older wolf never said anything about it.

Ava waited for half a beat before she continued. "Thank you for saving him."

Her cool hand brushed over his brow. Jackson turned into it. Her sweet scent was stronger than ever and he opened his mouth to taste it better.

"I don't care whether he lives or dies, honestly," Cunningham grunted. "I just—"

"You don't want Val to be upset. I saw how you constantly backed Val up in the battle. How you couldn't take your eyes off of her."

Jackson bolted upright. "WHAT?!"

Both Ava and Cunningham jumped. Ava put a hand to her heart, making a little whimpering noise. Jackson winced and looked at her apologetically, then turned a fierce glare on Cunningham.

"Stay away from my sister, Blizzard. I fucking mean it."

Cunningham met his eye. "I have no intentions of getting anywhere near her."

"Keep it that way." The last thing Val needed was some old man sniffing around. Not that he should be worried about this. Val had made it clear that she hated Cunningham more than once. Still, Jackson growled at him, just in case. "If you go near her I'll kill you."

Cunningham rolled his eyes. "Whatever. I'll go tell Typhoon you're awake again... unless you plan to faint again."

Jackson growled at him. The other wolf only grinned as he slipped out the door. Ava moved to sit beside him, and Jackson couldn't help himself. He pulled her into his arms and rolled over, pinning her beneath him.

"Hey, Kitten," he purred at her.

Ava let out a startled laugh. "You seem oddly energized."

"It's the venom." He moved to nibble her neck but stopped. Instead, he laid a hand on her stomach. "Is she..."

"The baby's fine. I wasn't in the fight all that much." Ava's arms moved up his to wrap around his neck. "God, Jackson. You scared me. Terrified me. I wanted to rip off your head myself when you went in to help Typhoon. I thought you were going to die helping that..." She sighed. "Actually, he's not that bad. He's been a perfect gentleman towards me."

Typhoon, a gentleman? Jackson snorted. "I'll believe it when I see it."

Typhoon's voice rumbled behind them. "And as much as I'd like to see this preggo porn play out, I don't have time for your sex life, Tornado. Get up."

The command rankled Jackson, but he did as he was ordered. His head spun a bit, but he managed to hold himself upright. He threw his shoulders back and stared Typhoon in the eye. Ava stood beside him, her hand clutched in his.

"So… how long do I have to recover before I have to kill you?" Jackson asked, his voice calm and even.

Typhoon rose a brow as he leaned against the doorframe. He folded his massive arms across his chest and smirked. "One, you'd never be able to kill me. Two, is that any way to speak to your alpha? Especially since I was generous enough to reinstate you as the alpha of the Coalfell chapter?"

Jackson's eyes widened. "Really?"

"Yeah. You saved my life out there. And I pay my debts." Typhoon frowned at him. "Convincing the vamps to release their claim on your mate was tricky, though. I expect you to pay double fees the next coming year. Oh, and I had to trade all lands between the lake and canyon to the vampires, so you lost a quarter of your territory. I hope she's worth it."

Jackson grinned. His wolf relaxed, now that Typhoon was... well, not on their side exactly but close enough. He took Ava's hand in his and brought her knuckles to his lips. "Oh, she is. So worth it."

Ava grinned back at him. "And you are worth it, too."

They kissed, earning a groan from Typhoon. Shaking his head, the other alpha left. Jackson let him go as he wrapped his arms around his mate, bringing her closer to him. She was here and safe... it was all he wanted.

***

Four Months Later

Jackson nuzzled Ava in the neck as she found her second release. He sunk deep inside of her, rocking in and out gently. Their sex life had certainly taken a turn since Lily was born. No more wild, loud nights. Now they kept quiet and kept it short but satisfying. Jackson found he needed to be extra careful with his mate. Her hormones were still a bit wild from pregnancy, meaning that sometimes she wasn't very sensitive at all, and other times felt raw after a few strokes.

"How's my girl?" he purred, nibbling at her ear.

She smiled and gave him that satisfied kitten look that drove him so wild every time he saw it. "I'm pretty good. Up for round three."

The baby monitor lit up then and they could hear the sound of Lily cooing in the next room, talking to herself as she woke up. Mornings often started like this. If they didn't get her quickly, though, she let them know that she had needs that weren't being filled—loudly. She was just as temperamental as her mother.

"I'll go get her," Jackson said, lifting himself off of Ava, who gave a soft whimper of discontent and frowned when he got up. He grinned at her.

"I'm sorry, kitten," he said.

She sighed.

"I know," she said. "Go get her and bring her in here. She needs to eat."

Jackson nodded, kissing Ava's forehead before he got up and went into the nursery where his baby daughter lay in her crib. As usual, he couldn't help but smile as he picked her up, looking at her eyes, the same color as his. Lily looked like Ava in almost every way, right down to the sweet roundness of her cheeks, but her eyes were his.

"Hi, Lil," Jackson said, wrapping her in a blanket, carrying her against his chest into the bedroom. Ava was sitting up in the bed, and her face lit up when Jackson brought her daughter to her, laying her in her mother's arms. Ava kissed the baby on the forehead, looking up at Jackson with a bright smile on her face.

"She's so beautiful," Ava said.

Jackson had to agree, though he couldn't take his eyes off of Ava's rapturous expression. At that moment, he knew that it was time—the moment he had been waiting for. His heart started to pound in his chest as he stood up.

"Where are you going?" she asked, frowning.

"Uh—I'm just going downstairs. To get coffee."

Ava raised her eyebrows. "Okay," she said. "You okay?"

"Yeah, I'm fine," Jackson said, brushing her off.

He cursed himself for being nervous. He wasn't a nervous person. Usually, he had his head on his shoulders. Missions were executed as he planned them. Always without a hitch. But for some reason, this was nagging at him, making him worry that his perfect moment would somehow go wrong.

Maybe because his plans always went out the window when it came to Ava.

Jackson went downstairs and put on the coffee, going into the front room and pulling a book out of the case. Behind the book was a little green velvet box. Jackson opened it to see the ring, glistening and untouched, inside. He shut it again and took a deep breath, putting it into his pocket. His heart raced as he poured two mugs of coffee and carefully carried them upstairs. Ava was laying on her back on the bed with the baby on her chest, stroking Lily's soft curls, humming to her in a sweet voice.

Lily fed eagerly, making greedy slurping noises.

"Why do you have that look on your face?" Ava asked, looking at him with one eyebrow raised.

"What look? I don't have a look," he said.

She laughed, leaning forward to kiss him as he handed her the mug. Ava took a sip. Jackson lay over her legs and kissed his daughter's head.

"What do you think, Lil?" he asked. "Do you think we should keep her? Is she a good mommy?"

Lily broke from Ava's breast to wave a hand in his face, then went right back to eating. Ava laughed.

"Have you been considering getting rid of me?" she asked.

Jackson shook his head, swallowing nervously as he reached into his pocket and handed her the box. Her lips parted, her mouth opening in surprise as she stared at the box.

"Open it," he urged.

She pulled it open, her eyes widening when she saw the ring inside. With a startled gasp, she dropped it again. Her mouth went into an 'o' as she looked up to stare into his eyes.

"I want you to marry me," he said to her. "I've known that's what I've wanted since—probably the first time I fought with you."

She chuckled. "You hated me."

"I never hated you. I always wanted you. And I will always want you," Jackson said to her, taking her hands as he snuggled Lily on his lap. He brought one up to kiss her fingers. "Please be my wife as well as my mate."

Ava stared at him for a moment before she bit her lip, smiling. She held out her hand and Jackson felt relief wash through him as he slipped the ring onto her finger. He leaned in and kissed her, shifting his body so that they were lying side by side with Lily nestled between them. He stared at his mate's face, drinking her in, knowing that every fight had been worth it to know that she would be his forever.

"Yes," she whispered. "Yes, I'll marry you. Gladly. More than gladly... I love you, my crazy wolf."

"And I love you, Kitten. I love you."

*****

THE END

Printed in Great Britain
by Amazon